Were Chronicles

PACK DAUGHTER

CRISSY SMITH

Pack Daughter
ISBN # 978-1-78651-954-2
©Copyright Crissy Smith 2018
Cover Art by Posh Gosh ©Copyright February 2018
Interior text design by Claire Siemaszkiewicz
Totally Bound Publishing

Totally Bound Publishing books by Crissy Smith

Were Chronicles
Pack Alpha
Pack Enforcer
Pack Territory
Pack Rogue
Pack Community
Pack Mates
Pack Daughter

Shifter Chronicles
Birds of Prey
Bear Claw
Eye of the Tiger
Coyote's Kiss
Wolf Pack
Lion's Claim

Bloodlines
Bite
Control
Embrace

What's Her Secret?
Designated Alpha

PACK
DAUGHTER

Dedication

This book is dedicated to my wonderful and
supportive family.
They have cheered me on from the sidelines and
always let me know that they believe in me.

Prologue

Becca Nelson blew her bangs from her eyes and surveyed the mess that the old community center had turned into. The fire had been extremely hot and had burned quickly. The community center was the latest casualty in a line of local buildings that had been targeted for arson. She raised her camera and started to click. In less than thirty seconds, she had dozens of photos — the building, still smoldering in the cool night air, the exhausted firefighters who had fought to save it, and the residents who looked on in horror and unease.

She'd already taken photos of the fire itself when it had still burned brightly. It was her job — she had to remain professional, even if the sight made her stomach hurt. The reality of what was happening right in front of her was devastating. Sighing, she lowered the camera again. "Damn it," she mumbled, unable to understand why anyone would torch the building that had been the centerpiece for so many wonderful memories.

Becca had attended her senior prom there, watched several of her friends perform mating ceremonies, and had even planned one for herself. Her ceremony had never taken place, but the memories associated with it still made her smile. Now, her heart ached with the loss.

The fourth building burned to the ground. What would be next? Who might be hurt or killed? Those questions haunted her and every resident of Riverwood. For over a month, the city where she'd lived her entire life had slowly been taken from her. The first fire, a small one compared to tonight's, had been on the edge of town — an old farmhouse that had been converted into the town's museum. When tourists wished to learn more about the first known wolf shifter community, they could stop by and pick up brochures and information.

With the help of the Alpha Council, the city of Riverwood, once on the brink of extinction, was now a hot, must-see tourist site.

Riverwood, with a population of over three thousand residents, had barely been surviving before the shifter world had gone public. Now, three months after the announcement, visitors flocked to the once-forgotten town. Businesses that had been boarded up and abandoned had been remodeled and now thrived. Families who had believed they would have to leave their homes to find work were now proud and happy in their hometown.

The changes had come quickly, but had breathed new life into the Pack.

Then the fires had started. First the museum, then the school house, followed by the bank and now the community center.

Becca turned and walked back to her Tahoe, still feeling the weight of the scene heavy on her shoulders.

She packed away her things and turned to look one last time at the building. She'd need to get the photos printed for both the police and the newspaper. It would be a long night and she didn't look forward to seeing what she had captured — a memory that would forever be imprinted on the community.

As she stared back at the building, two bodies broke away from the small group of firefighters and made their way over to her. She offered a small smile to her two best friends when they reached her.

Kenny Moore and Todd Wilkins looked exhausted. Sweat soaked their T-shirts, their eyes were dark and serious, and they appeared almost dead on their feet.

Kenny shook his head. "I can't believe this," he said. "Again."

She would have hugged him, but she didn't think she could offer much comfort right then without breaking down herself. Todd clasped a hand on Kenny's shoulder and squeezed. Kenny visibly relaxed. They loved one another, had committed themselves, although they had never taken the last step. She was a little jealous of them but had always supported them. The two of them had gotten her through the roughest patches of her life. Up until now, the future had always been bright. The recent destruction had taken its toll on all of them, though.

"Anything?" she asked, nodding toward the building. It was good having friends working with the fire department and police. Becca normally tried to remain objective with the photos she took. Things were changing, though. Her town didn't feel safe any longer.

Todd dropped his hand and turned to look at the community center that was now no more than rubble on the ground. "Same as before. It was too late by the time we got here. All we could do was stop the fire from spreading. It's a complete loss."

"They keep getting closer to downtown," Becca admitted her fear. "And I can't help but wonder, then what? The entire town or Alpha property could be next."

Todd shook his head. "I don't want to find out. We have to stop this. So far, no one's been hurt but…"

Neither she nor Kenny wanted to be the one to finish the thought. They were all thinking it, but to say it out loud? No one wanted to be the one to go there.

"Yeah," she said instead.

"We gotta head back. You staying in town or at your dad's?" Todd asked.

Becca thought it over. Her apartment was closer, but she needed her Pack. To see her father and know he was okay. Plus, having the other shifters close by helped calm her wolf. "I'll stay at the cottage."

Todd released a breath. "Good. We'll be over when our shift is finished."

She exchanged one-armed hugs with both men as they tried to keep her from getting dirty. They all needed the contact—a brush of a hand or a light caress could still the anxiety inside. She watched them walk back to the fire engine, jump up and disappear inside. Then she glanced around the crowd that was slowly drifting away.

Someone had to have seen something. There was no way whoever did this could keep from standing out in town. There were so many questions but no answers. That wasn't her job, though. She had to rely on the police to figure it out. Or at least wait until she spoke to her father. The Pack Alpha had the authority to stick his nose into the town's business.

She slammed the rear hatch closed and dragged her tired body to the driver's side. She wanted to get home. Becca started the engine then, without looking back, drove down the street.

It was quiet now. Without the sirens of the emergency vehicles, the silence seemed odd. A bustling street turned into a dead zone.

They'd rebuild. It was what a community did, but things wouldn't be the same.

Even with the money that flowed in from the tourists, this financial hit would hurt the Pack. Becca knew she should be grateful about no one getting hurt. The emotional damage that they all felt was as upsetting, though. A strong town being torn down brick by brick wasn't fair.

Anger began to replace the despair. Yes, she wanted the fury to fill her.

Becca was the Alpha's daughter — it was time she took care of her family. The Pack was that, her family, extended aunts, uncles, and cousins. If there was a monster out there ready to bring them down, she would fight. This was going to end.

Chapter One

Mike Jackson strolled into the sheriff's office of Lawton, New Mexico, with a smile. It hadn't been that long ago that he'd arrived in town to help his best friend RJ Cross as RJ's brother, Dylan, was accepting the position of Pack Alpha.

Now, Lawton was like a second home to him. Actually, if he was being honest, he felt more comfortable there than with his own family. Here, Mike was accepted and understood. He'd never found that feeling until he'd joined the military where he had met the people he would love for the rest of his life.

He waved to the pretty receptionist and tilted his head toward Brandon Stratton's office. "Is he in?"

The receptionist smiled back at him. They'd flirted back and forth, but the petite woman didn't do it for him. Mike enjoyed the chase, but it wasn't very often that he followed through with bedding the female who'd caught his attention. The last time he'd been with anyone had been right after RJ's mating ceremony. Now, *that* had been a good night. The woman he'd hooked up still had his imagination going wild when he was alone with his hand.

"He's waiting for you. Go on back." The receptionist sat forward, giving Mike a good view down her low top.

Mike inclined his head and made his way to the back office. He'd been summoned, so he'd have to return later and finish flirting.

Brandon Stratton, the sheriff deputy and second in command of the Pack, reclined back in his chair with his eyes closed. Mike grinned evilly. *Oh, perfect.*

Mike knocked loudly and stifled a laugh as the other man jerked in his chair.

"Damn it, man!" Brandon groused.

Mike continued to chuckle. "If I knew you were lazing around, I would have gotten here sooner. Did crime take a vacation? Or is this what the sheriff does all day?"

"Screw you, Jackson," Brandon said. "I've been working double shifts and I'm tired."

"Oh, poor baby." Mike clucked his tongue. "Maybe you need to hire a few more deputies."

"You won't take the job," Brandon complained.

Yeah, Mike wasn't quite ready to commit to anything at the moment.

"But I'm not going to badger you about it. Not today, anyway." When Brandon stood and offered a hand, Mike shook it readily. He hadn't expected to become such good friends with Brandon. Not after all the drama that had taken place several months ago. But Brandon had proven himself to be a great asset to the Pack.

When Mike had first arrived in town, Brandon was considering challenging for the Pack Alpha position. He didn't want the job, but other members of the Pack had been putting a lot of pressure on him to not let a stranger take over. Luckily, Brandon's sister had stepped in and, with help from RJ, they had brought both men together and had avoided a challenge between the two of them.

"Good to see you, man. Thanks for coming," Brandon told him.

He took a seat in front of the desk while Brandon walked around and closed the office door. He waited until Brandon had settled back into his chair before he spoke. "Sounded important."

Mike had been traveling back from Texas, where he had been visiting Casey, another member of his old military unit. He'd planned on stopping in and seeing RJ even before he got Brandon's call.

"It is." Brandon pulled a file from his bottom drawer. "You've heard about the threats to the Packs that went public?"

Mike nodded. It was one of the reasons he'd been in Coyote Bluff. His old unit commander and his mate, the feline Prince, were concerned about the new threat to the shifters. For the first few weeks since the announcement, the excitement about there being shifters had been top news. But as time passed, more and more people—humans—started to see shifters as a threat.

Shifter communities that had chosen to be open now had to deal with some heavy backlash in the form of threats.

"Riverwood, California. Last night was the fourth fire in less than a month. Before each fire, a letter is sent to the Alpha. 'Surrender the Pack and land or the town will burn,'" Brandon informed him.

Mike opened the file. The Pack was located in northern California, not far from his own Pack.

Population over three thousand. The first known organized community of shifters.

It had become common for shifter species to live and work together, depending on one another to survive. But that wasn't how it had always been. Long ago, the shifters had lived by the rule that only the strongest survived. The Pack Alpha in Riverwood had known the shifters would never last if they kept killing each other. He'd started the first community that welcomed shifters to live in harmony.

Because of the success of his idea, shifter communities now thrived all over the world. As years passed, the Alpha position had been passed down to the next generation, but the honor that came with being the first community never faded.

The current Pack Alpha, Jim Nelson, had decided to go public because, over the years, the pack had fallen on hard times. He'd approached the Alpha Council and received approval to brand the title of the first known shifter community. It had sounded like a good plan to Mike. And it had seemed to work. The entire town had grown. Mike had always supported the decision to go public and had agreed that own Alpha should take that step.

He flipped through the pages and read the report that looked like a copy of the police investigation. The photos of the fires showed him more. Someone was out to ruin the town.

"The fires are always at places that the town depends on. And they are getting closer to the downtown district and homes," Brandon said.

"Anyone hurt?"

"No, luckily all buildings have been empty at the time. But the concern is that if they don't get what they want, that'll change."

"Do we know who *they* are?"

"No. And no instructions on how they want the Alpha to 'surrender' his Pack," Brandon said. "The demand is bullshit. They want to hurt people. But without knowing who's involved, they don't know whether to look at locals or tourists. That's where you come in."

Mike lifted an eyebrow. He knew what was coming. "And what do you want with me?"

Brandon sighed. "Alpha Nelson has reached out to the council and asked for help. Dylan was approached to see if he had any ideas."

"And?"

"Dylan and RJ thought you'd be a good man for the job."

Now they were getting somewhere. "What kind of job?"

Brandon grinned. "Recon. Like what you did with the unit."

"And how do you know what I did with the unit?" Mike questioned, grinning in turn.

The unit he'd belonged to had been made up of all shifters. Several different shifter species. He and RJ were both wolves, but they also had felines and bird shifters as part of the team. "And how is this even remotely the same?"

"Hey." Bandon held up his hands. "Blame the Cross brothers. I'm the contact to Alpha Nelson, but sending you was their idea. Something about you drifting around lately and unable to settle?"

He nodded. He'd been a little lost since he'd left the military and he had always enjoyed helping others.

"Also you should know that our family has been close to the Nelson Pack for years. Nikki and the Alpha's daughter are real close. If you don't do it, she might not be happy and you know what that means."

Mike grinned. "If Nikki's not happy, then RJ's not happy."

"None of us want to deal with him when he gets all pouty and irritated. He's like a four year old."

That statement was too true. RJ Cross might appear to be the big bad biker to the outside world, but he was a big baby. He was also completely in love with his mate. It was both sweet and sickening to witness. "I don't mind helping out," Mike offered. "And I don't want anything to happen to this Pack. I'll go."

Brandon clapped his hands together. "That's great! I was hoping to be able to tell Alpha Nelson something today. This is a big load off my shoulders."

Mike shrugged. "It's not like I had any big plans, anyway."

He'd been headed home, even though he knew he wouldn't be there for long. Mike couldn't seem to stay in one place. So much had happened in the last year. It had started with the kidnapping of the feline Prince, then the long mission of getting him back, before they left the military. Casey and RJ finding their mates. Then the shifters going public...

His whole life, he had moved from one purpose to another.

The last few months seemed like he was cruising. And he didn't like it all. Yeah, RJ was right, Mike was drifting. He'd even thought about going back to the military. He hadn't shared that thought with anyone else, though. Now that he wasn't tied down every day, he wasn't sure what he wanted to do.

Maybe this assignment would help him decide. It would be nice to have a purpose once again, anyway.

He stood and offered his hand to Brandon. "I'd like to see RJ while I'm in town, but I can leave tonight."

Brandon came around the desk and threw an arm over his shoulder. "Nah, man, we're having a cookout for the family at the Alpha house tonight. Come along with RJ and Nikki and leave in the morning. I'll let Alpha Nelson know to expect you tomorrow."

Good food, cold beer and his friends. He wasn't going to pass up a night with like that. "Sounds good to me," Mike agreed.

He left Brandon at the office door, stepped out into the warm early evening air and looked around the main street of the small town. There weren't many people walking around, which only added to the small-town feel.

The community was friendly and anyone who did pass waved to him. He glanced down the street and saw that RJ's tattoo shop still had the open sign lit up. It had taken time, but from what RJ had told him, people were finally coming around to his shop. He was even getting quite a few out-of-town appointments once word got out that he did custom mate tattoos.

Mike was happy for his friend. RJ had an amazing talent. He had done every one of Mike's tattoos. He started in the direction of RJ's shop, taking his time. He still had the file for the California Pack under his arm and he wanted to talk it over with RJ. He would do whatever he could to help the wolves in need.

He pulled open the door of the tattoo parlor and was not surprised to see RJ sitting in a chair with his mate Nikki Stratton straddling his lap.

Luckily, they still had their clothes on. The two new mates seemed to spend a lot of time in the process of undressing each other.

RJ glanced up when Mike walked in and grinned at him. "Hey, man! We were talking about you."

Mike smirked. "I hope it was before Nikki had her hand under your shirt or it might get a little awkward."

RJ laughed and Nikki blushed, removing said hand from under RJ's black T-shirt. She started to slide off RJ's lap, but he caught her easily.

"Where do you think you're going?"

She pinched RJ and was able to escape. "I told you I had things to do. You've gotta stop distracting me."

RJ pouted. Actually pouted and Mike couldn't hold back his roll of laughter.

Nikki shook her head and grabbed her messenger bag from the counter. She stopped close to him and kissed his cheek. "It's good to see you, Mike."

He looked over to the woman he now felt was like a sister to him. "You, too, honey."

"You staying for a little while?"

He shook his head. "Just tonight. I have to head out in the morning to help another Pack that's having issues."

She sighed. "I thought we were doing the right thing going public. I never thought it would scare so many people."

"Hey!" RJ came up behind her. "It is a good thing. People fear what they don't know. It'll get better."

"I hope so," she stated.

Mike hoped so, too.

"But I do have to run. I need to finish the potato salad and cobbler for tonight. I'll get your room ready, too, Mike."

They took good care of him, always welcomed him whenever he was in town, even opening their house to let him use the spare bedroom. "Don't go to any trouble, I'll be here one night," he told her.

She waved him off. "It's no trouble for family." She kissed RJ one more time then sidestepped out of his reach when he grabbed her for another. "Stay out of trouble, boys," she called then left them alone.

RJ threw his arm around Mike and walked him farther into the shop. "So you're heading out to California then? I thought you'd be perfect for it."

Mike elbowed his friend. "Really? I hadn't caught that by what you told Brandon about me."

RJ motioned to one of the big chairs and Mike sat while his friend grabbed two beers from the mini fridge. "I'm worried about you, man," RJ confessed.

Mike glanced up, shocked. "Why? There's nothing wrong with me!"

RJ held a hand up. "You're not happy. Do you think I can't tell when something is going on with my best friend?"

Mike sighed. "It's fine, man. I'm trying to find my niche."

"Yeah," RJ agreed. "I understand. You're thinking about joining again, aren't you?"

Mike took a sip of his beer and relaxed into the chair. He wasn't surprised RJ had picked up on how he was feeling, even if he wasn't ready to talk about it yet. But he knew his best friend, and RJ wouldn't leave him alone until they did talk.

"Yes," he admitted.

RJ nodded. "Thought so. I hate to think about you going back in without my being there to watch your back. I'll support you no matter what you decide, but I want you to do this first."

"Well, I'll do what I can. You know that."

"Yeah, plus...the Alpha's daughter...?" RJ's gaze twinkled with mischief.

"Daughter?"

"Yeah, you've met her," RJ said.

"When?" He tried to place what the Alpha's daughter looked like, but he couldn't think of anyone. He was from around that area but didn't have a clue who this chick was.

"When you were getting drunk with her at my mating ceremony," RJ quipped.

"*Becca?*"

"That would be her," RJ confirmed.

Holy shit, Becca had been hot and they had gotten drunk. It was been fun. He'd even followed her back to her room where they'd spent the entire night learning each other's bodies.

"Oh, yeah, you remember her," RJ teased. His best friend didn't know that he'd had sex with her. Mike was going to keep it that way. But now more than before he was going to fix things in California.

"Nikki wants to go down there herself and it's all I can do to keep my mate away from the danger. So I suggested you."

"What, you wanted me to look out for Nikki's friend?" Mike asked, amused. "Meaning you can keep Nikki here."

RJ huffed then smiled. "I can't have an unhappy mate. I almost had to lock her up to keep her from going up after the second fire. She was ready to jump on a plane."

Mike could imagine that fight. Nikki was one of the most stubborn, hard-headed females he'd ever met. He really did like her.

"Stop smirking," RJ grumbled. "You wait until you find your mate. You'll see then."

Mike smacked the finger RJ waved at him. "I don't know that I will be so—"

"Don't say it," RJ threatened.

"Whipped," Mike responded.

RJ flipped him off, but had a huge grin on his face.

* * * *

Becca tried not to roll her eyes at her dad, but as the lecture went on and on, it was getting harder. If her father's Beta, Eric, the Pack Enforcer, Adrian, and the head of security for the Pack, her best friend, Kenny, hadn't been in the room, she was sure she would have already. But even she knew that now was no time to push her dad. She could admit that the threats made to the Pack put them in danger. Her own knowledge of the fires broke her heart, but she was more than capable of taking care of herself.

"Are you listening to me, Becca?" her father yelled.

Becca snapped back to attention. She'd drifted off in the middle of his latest rant. "Yes, Dad, but I don't need protection. I do not need some wolf from another Pack to come up here and keep an eye on me," she argued for what felt like the millionth time in the last few days. "There's no reason to think anyone will come after me."

Her father shook his head. "He's already on his way. And I want you to listen to him. He had better not report back to me that you are not cooperating. He's not here to keep an eye on you, as you said. He'll also try to help us figure out what is going on. To catch the people responsible once and for all. We need the help."

Becca sighed. "Fine." She met her dad's gaze. She had never deliberately defied him. And he knew it. They were close. As close as any daughter and dad could be.

It had been the two of them after her mom had been killed by a hunter one night when she'd shifted and gone for a run. Her dad never got over losing his mate but had always been there for Becca. Had been her everything—father, mother and Alpha.

When the council had sent a representative to talk to him about the shifter world going public, her father didn't have to even think about it. After the way he'd lost his mate, he supported the council one hundred percent. Plus it had been horrible seeing his Pack struggle to survive. There wasn't much the Pack could offer being so far away from civilization. It had been a great idea to bring the tourists in. Now that might be what would destroy them.

"We'll let him keep an eye on things while we try to figure out what is going on," her father reiterated.

"Do you really think someone from our Pack is involved with the fires?" she asked. Becca couldn't believe that someone from the Pack she'd been born into would ever do something so...disgusting. They'd known from the start that the Alpha would go public. They had been there when his mate had been killed.

Becca couldn't fathom one of the Pack members being involved.

Her dad shook his head sadly. "I don't want to believe it. But we do have to be prepared for it."

"What about you?" she questioned, leaning forward on the couch. "You have to be the biggest target. Take down the Alpha and the Pack will shortly follow."

Her dad pressed his lips together, but she still saw the flash of amusement in his eyes before he could hide it. "I have increased my security, as well as the security around the property. I've also sent word out that anyone who doesn't feel comfortable staying in their own homes is welcome. I opened the guest houses."

Becca smiled in pride. Her father might stick to his guns, but he would also make sure that his Pack was taken care of. She was so proud of him. The Pack wasn't the easiest to run, but he did it with love and strength.

A knock on the door interrupted any further discussion. Eric stood and glanced at his watch.

"That should be the guy the council and Brandon Stratton sent."

Becca leaned forward so she could see the door while Eric opened it.

And almost fell right off the couch.

The man who entered was that breathtaking. Dark hair, wide shoulders, a tan, pleasant face with a goatee — and she knew him. Oh, shit, did she know him. He screamed military and she could see why the council would have thought he'd be a good fit with the Pack. The man glanced around, taking everything in while scanning the room.

She flushed, remembering how much of a pain she'd been when her dad had told her about him. Because looking at him now, she could think of several activities they might have fun at. Ever since meeting Mike at Nikki's mating ceremony, she hadn't forgotten about him.

Her father stood and she followed suit.

The man shook Eric's hand before moving to the Alpha.

"Alpha Nelson, it's a pleasure to meet you. I'm sorry it's under these circumstances, though."

Her father nodded. "Yes, but I am glad to finally meet you. I have heard wonderful things about you and the work you did for the military."

Her dad cleared his throat and she realized she was practically undressing with her eyes the man in front of her in a room with her dad and his two top men.

She blushed but held out her hand. "Good to see you again, Mike," she said, relieved when her voice came out normally. She wanted to purr for him. To rub up against him. She felt her wolf part ripple with excitement on the inside.

"Hello, Becca. You, too. Nikki sends her love," he greeted.

"You two know each other?" her father asked. Becca did not miss the laughter in his voice.

"He's best friends with Nikki's mate. We were both part of the ceremony."

Her dad put an arm around her shoulder and steered her back toward the couch. She also caught Eric's and Kenny's amused expressions. "How convenient."

She snorted. Okay, she might have been pretty obvious about her attraction to Mike, but she didn't need to be teased. She hadn't expected to ever see the man again. They hadn't even exchanged phone numbers.

"Let's have a seat and we'll get you settled into a room, Mike," her dad stated. "I'm sure you'd like to get settled after traveling all day."

Mike sat in one of the chairs across from her dad's desk, so Kenny sat next to her on the couch.

"Real smooth there," Kenny teased.

She elbowed him, already embarrassed. "I was surprised."

"And horny."

"I hate you," she muttered.

He covered up his chuckle with a cough when her dad glanced over at them.

Becca shrugged before pointing at Kenny. Kenny smacked her hand away. Her father turned back to Mike, but he was smiling.

She listened in as her dad caught Mike up on everything that had happened in the last several weeks. Mike listened intently to her father, so she enjoyed looking at him. It wasn't that she was desperate for male company or anything, but it had been a long time since she had felt a connection like she'd had with him.

Plus, the way he'd made love to her had rocked her world. He'd been dominant but gentle. Becca still thought about the one time they'd had, often.

"Want to tell me how well you know him?" Kenny whispered.

"It's him," she admitted. "The guy I told you I met."

"I figured that out on my own."

"I can't believe he's here," she said.

"Well, he was as excited to see you as you were him," Kenny whispered.

"What do you mean?"

"How'd you miss his erection as soon as he touched you? The pheromones in the room almost choked me," Kenny said.

"I'm going to choke you if you don't shut up," she warned.

"Nah, Todd tries but my gag—"

Becca pinched his thigh as hard as she could. This was not the time for him to bring up his and Todd's sex life. Especially when the man she'd been fantasizing about was a few feet away.

Mike Jackson was in her childhood home.

How had the tragic events of the past few weeks led to this?

He sat stiffly, listening to her father. It was obvious that Mike cared. His arrival in her territory showed that he was a good man. If she hadn't been attracted to him before, his willingness to come help would have pushed her over the edge.

Becca licked her lips, planning how to get him alone, very soon.

Chapter Two

Mike tried to concentrate on the Alpha, but his attention was on the man's daughter. She sat over in the corner next to the shifter who'd been introduced as the head of security. They sat too close for Mike's comfort and he wondered if they were an item. He quickly dismissed that idea as he remembered how she'd checked him out. She must still feel the connection that had been present during their first meeting.

He tried to hide his reaction when they'd touched, but his cock was throbbing in need. Luckily the Alpha and other shifters in the room had been amused and not taken offense.

When the Alpha shared his concern that he or his daughter might be a target, Mike could barely hold back his growl. No one was going to hurt Becca or her family. He accepted the file that Alpha Nelson pushed across the desk at him and glanced through it. There were pictures and profiles of eight men inside. It was more detailed than the information he'd gotten from Brandon.

"These are a few Pack members who I think could be involved. Kenny worked up the files, so any questions, get on to him."

Mike nodded. It looked to be good work.

"Kenny also has a few friends he trusts who have agreed to come here and discreetly check them out."

Mike understood what the Alpha didn't say — men who they probably would not see. They'd be doing their search out of the view of public.

"While you're here, we would like you to introduce yourself to them and get your own feel."

Mike tilted his head in acknowledgment. The Alpha was doing everything that could be done. He was thorough and organized. Mike appreciated the care he was putting into taking care of his Pack. A good Alpha was sitting before him. Mike knew many men who led well and Becca's father was right on top of the list. It helped ease some of his tension.

"But first priority is Becca." He waved over to his daughter and Mike finally had the chance to look at her again. Which he didn't mind at all.

She couldn't have been taller than five three or so. She had long black hair tied away from her face. He couldn't say what exactly had drawn his attention to her that first time — the warm smile, the happiness in her gaze, or the way she carried herself. For whatever reason, he'd been instantly attracted. He was also aware how smooth her hands had been on his chest. The way she'd hummed while sucking on his cock. Or the tightness of her pussy when he'd been buried deep inside her.

Fuck, if he didn't stop remembering, he was going to have to excuse himself to go jack off in the bathroom. Or find the nearest flat surface and take her again.

Becca squirmed in her seat as the attention turned to her. "And you, Dad. You're still the biggest target."

The Alpha smiled. Mike liked the obvious caring between daughter and father. He wanted to help the Pack and not because of his attraction to Becca. He felt comfortable here. Much like when he was in Lawton.

"I'd like to look around a little bit before it gets late," Mike said to the Alpha.

The Alpha nodded. "Kenny will give you a tour of the property. If you have any questions, he should be able to answer them, or I'll be working in here for a while yet."

Mike stood and shook hands with the Alpha once again. He was glad that Kenny would be showing him around. He wanted to know more about these *friends* that were looking into the Pack. Plus, he seemed close to Becca. Now that he had a personal stake in this business, he'd see what he could get out of Kenny about the woman who interested him.

He followed Kenny but glanced over his shoulder at Becca and was pleased that she continued to watch him. He sent her a small smile, which she returned. Yeah, they'd have time to catch up later. She wanted it as much as he did.

Mike and Kenny walked down a long hallway, through what looked like a living room then out of a glass patio door. This Alpha residence was homey and comfortable. He'd been raised in and had visited other Alpha properties that had shown off money and prestige. Mike didn't like those homes because they weren't homes. a way for the Alpha to show off. Places like this were where he was at ease.

"We have more territory than a lot of communities. Everyone is pretty spread out here. It gives us more privacy and independence than some of the Packs I've been to. Most everyone appreciates that," Kenny told him.

Mike understood what he was saying. Since his friends had started to settle down with their mates, he had got an up-close view of how many Packs functioned.

"There are no gates, no walls, to keep the Pack separate," Kenny continued. "Alpha Nelson likes to stay available."

"That also makes it more difficult to protect him," Mike noted.

"Yeah," Kenny agreed. "It's been one of the biggest issues I've had to deal with. My Alpha is taking the threats seriously, but he still refuses to even consider staying inside or having a fence built to help with security."

"He wants to show strength," Mike commented.

"That, and he would actually prefer for someone to come after him than target anyone else in his Pack. The destruction of the buildings is hurting the Pack. But there are only so many buildings. When will they go after the Pack members?" Kenny added.

Mike respected that. It showed the Alpha cared about his people. He also agreed with the statement.

"We've had eight families move into the guest houses. All have small children we're concerned about. What if these monsters go after the kids?"

A growl rumbled through Mike's chest—his wolf wanting to protect. It was an instinct that had always helped him in the past. While most shifters only ran or changed form maybe once a week or even less often, Mike shifted almost every day. His wolf was strong and he wanted to keep in shape, in both forms.

They walked around, going over weak spots and where trouble might come from. Kenny wouldn't say much about his friends who were working in the shadows, that they were wolf shifters and had been in the military. That they would watch out for everyone. Mike could understand why Kenny was keeping things close. He knew the brotherhood that came with a team. It was the same for him, Casey, RJ and Jesse. But Mike hated not having all the info.

When Kenny led Mike to the bedroom that would be his for the length of his stay, his bags were waiting for him on the bed. Now, he wished he'd picked up some better clothes at a mall or something. At the mating ceremony, he'd worn a suit. The days before when he'd seen Becca, he'd also been dressed up, due to so many formal gatherings. He'd only packed jeans and T-shirts for this trip, though. Nothing to impress her with.

"I'd like to shift and run later. Will that be a problem?" he asked. It was proper etiquette to ask while in another territory.

"No, the good thing about us is that you can shift anytime. We are so far from anyone who isn't a shifter that no one will think twice about seeing a wolf. Of course, nowadays people would love to see it, but no one comes this far out. Not even lost tourists."

"Good," Mike responded. "It'll help to also see the property as my wolf."

"There might be a couple of the cottages you'll want to check out," Kenny said.

"Oh?"

"Becca stays in one of them." Kenny winked.

Well, he guessed Kenny knew a little bit about them. "I'll keep that in mind." He wanted to ask him more about her but decided against it. At least until he knew what their relationship was. Or if she had a relationship with anyone around there. Mike was only there for a limited time and he didn't want to mess up anything for her. Now that there was space between the two of them Mike had some control over his hormones.

"The kitchen is always open. Help yourself to anything you want. Alpha Nelson has someone come in and cook breakfast from seven to eight, lunch from eleven to one and dinner is at five. But the fridge is always stocked with sandwiches or something if you miss a meal or want a snack."

"I appreciate it," Mike told Kenny and they shook hands.

"Oh!" Kenny pulled out a sheet of paper from his back pocket. "Here are some phone numbers for the Pack. If you need anything, give me a holler."

Mike closed the door after Kenny had left and walked around the room, familiarizing himself with his surroundings. It was a nice room. Deep cherrywood furniture that was both sturdy and comforting. His room had a king-sized bed, a dresser with a TV on it, and two end tables. There was an attached bathroom, so Mike picked up his small tote and set it inside the small space. He would shower after he'd shifted.

He wandered over to the window and pulled back the curtains. One thing was for sure, he had a gorgeous view of the mountains. It was colder than what he was used to, but Mike found the territory to be very welcoming. He was still itching for a run, so he decided to go ahead. Mike quietly left his room and strode down the hall to the same patio door he and Kenny had exited through earlier. In the short time he'd been inside, the temperature had dropped by several degrees. His wolf wouldn't mind, though.

Mike went in the opposite direction of the guest houses—he didn't want to meet up with anyone else then—past a swimming pool, a small but well-kept playground for the children, and what looked like another guest house, a little bigger than the ones he'd seen earlier.

"Nice," he murmured. This territory was large indeed. Mike moved through the thick dense trees until he felt the calmness of the woods. It was even chillier once he was surrounded by the large foliage and he started to strip. It wouldn't matter for long, though— his built-in fur coat would take care of any lingering coldness. He stood completely naked and took a deep breath. Faint traces of other wolves were apparent, but he didn't sense anyone around right then. He dropped to his hands and knees and began his shift.

His transformation was effortless. One minute, he was human, and the next, wolf. His vision was different when in his animal form. It was also easier to use his other senses.

The scent of fresh foliage, the breeze that ruffled his fur, even the songs of the birds above him were louder. Mike loved nature.

He shook his entire body hard before trotting off. There was so much to explore.

Recon was his specialty. He could stalk around an area without anyone seeing him if he wanted. Mike figured that he could spend a good few hours checking things out before returning to the Alpha house to make phone calls.

Right now, it was him and the territory.

* * * *

Becca finished folding the last of her laundry, placed the shirts in a pile on top of the dryer and sighed. It had been a stressful few weeks that seemed to be catching up with her. The appearance of Mike Jackson had made it hit home that they were in trouble.

What she couldn't figure out was, why come after her Pack? Was it the publicity they had received?

Their Pack wasn't the biggest, the richest or the strongest. It also wasn't the weakest. They were more in the middle. She'd met several other Packs that would have made more sense to direct the threats and attacks toward.

One of the strongest Packs was in West Texas and the Alpha Gage Wolf was one of the best-known shifters in the world. There was even talk about him joining the Alpha council when his father retired. And Alpha Wolf was mated and had a young child, who he would protect with his life—with everything he had. So maybe whoever was doing this was smart by not going after that Pack.

But then there was Lamont's Pack. Lamont's youngest son, Tony, was the head of the committee that had been instrumental in the shifters going public. Going after them made more sense than messing with a Pack located in the middle of nowhere and without a lot of power in the shifter world.

It frustrated her to no end that what might have saved the Pack—public knowledge of them being the first in existence—could be their downfall.

And what she was trying to avoid thinking about was how Mike had made her feel. Again. After their previous experience she'd not been able to move past like she should have been.

Becca had always thought that she'd found the man she was supposed to be with for the rest of her life. After she'd been left Becca had rarely indulged in flirting much less sex. She hadn't been able to resist Mike, though.

Watching Mike with his best friend RJ had been fun. At times, they'd acted like a couple of teenagers, and at others, their close bond was obvious. There was no question that they'd both been military. What Becca hadn't expected was the humor they shared.

She appreciated a man with a sense of humor.

Life was too serious most of the time. Living as a shifter was never easy. Even before they'd come out to the public.

When half a person's soul belonged to an animal, instinct was a part of them.

Becca trusted her instincts. That was why when Mike had started flirting with her, she'd been receptive. A little alcohol for courage and *bam* they were hot and heavy for each other.

She grabbed the clean clothes and went to the bedroom. Putting the laundry away, she caught sight of the curtains blowing in the breeze. She'd left the window cracked, loving the smell of fresh air traveling through her house.

Becca stepped closer and gazed into the night.

It was home. Even though she didn't live full-time on the property, she still had her own cottage. Becca rarely took long assignments or ones far away anymore and never considered living anywhere else.

Luckily, she had the support of her father. No matter what happened, she was always welcome back. It had been a hard few years after her mother had been killed, but because of that she had a supportive relationship with her father, one she knew many of her friends were envious of. When she'd been younger, she'd often wondered if her dad would still be around when she was an adult. So many wolves followed their mate in death. But her dad was a strong and wonderful leader and she was proud that his Pack always came first.

He'd always supported her career choices. When she had started out and had taken jobs in different parts of the globe, he'd worried, but always accepted her home again. Being a nature photographer and photojournalist, she spent a lot of time in isolated places surrounded by animals and living things. It was a beautiful world out there. but it could be scary, too. Over the last few years, she'd moved away from being a photojournalist and concentrated more on nature photography. She wasn't going to let someone take that away from her or the Pack.

Inspired by the chance to spend some time in her own territory, she grabbed her camera off the desk and headed outside. She snagged the hoodie hanging on the hook by the front door. Nights always got cold quick around there.

Becca breathed in the scent of home while she traveled through the thick foliage. She knew the area like the back of her hand. She'd played in the woods as a child and had spent every summer swimming in the creek not far away. She decided she'd walk to the creek and take a few pictures of the moon reflecting from the water.

The area was alive around her. She could hear movement in the trees above her head as well as a far-off howl. She shivered with excitement, feeling free and comfortable.

As she came around the footpath leading to the creek, she picked up another scent and her body instantly went on alert. An unfamiliar wolf shifter was near. She slowed her steps and crouched once the creek came into view. She was downwind from the unknown wolf so if she didn't make any noise, she shouldn't be spotted.

The large animal was one of the most beautiful she had ever seen. He—and it was most definitely a he—dipped his head and lapped slowly at the water.

It was a picture that she could not resist. She raised the camera and clicked off several shots before the wolf lifted his head and looked right at her. She snapped one last picture. That picture—the wolf's head up, shoulders back—was as close to perfect as she'd ever taken.

Now that she'd been seen, there was no point in ducking back down. She stood from her hiding place and stepped forward. The wolf dropped down to the ground, still watching her.

She didn't feel any threat from the animal and made her way over. It wasn't until she was several feet away that she knew for sure that the shifter in front of her was Mike Jackson. He still carried the same sensual scent but with a stronger masculine smell as a wolf.

He pawed the ground when she paused.

"Out for a run, huh?" she asked the animal.

While shifters did keep their human intelligence in their other form, it wasn't like he could talk back. He tilted his head to the side and she grinned. Becca strode a little closer before sitting down close to him.

They hadn't shifted together before, so she was cautious. Some shifters didn't like anyone but their own Pack members seeing them changed. She didn't think Mike would be that way, but she needed for him to make a move first.

Mike crawled closer to her and she reached toward him until she felt his soft, thick fur under her hand. She gave his head a good hard scratch. He plopped down and turned onto his side.

Oh, yeah, he was fully male. She'd already seen what a nice-sized cock he had as a human, but as a wolf he was still impressive. Becca rubbed and patted his side until he stood and shook. His dark gaze met hers in question. Then he nudged her gently. She could only guess what he wanted.

"Okay, turn around and I'll shift," she told him.

He sat, still looking right at her.

"Oh, no!" She waved a finger at his nose. "I know damn well you can understand me and see fine. Turn around."

He gave what she could only describe as a wolf sigh but did turn and face the other direction. Yeah, it might be ridiculous, but she wasn't going to undress with a wolf watching her. Even if he'd already seen everything. She stripped fast, placing her camera on top of her folded clothes before she started to transform into her wolf.

It took a minute, but eventually fur covered her body instead of skin, instantly warming her.

Becca was smaller than him. But, then again, she had expected to be. She gazed at him with her wolf eyes and felt a longing deep inside.

Mike still had his back turned, so she stretched and without warning bumped into him.

He turned, surprised.

She nipped at his flank and took off running. She loved the feeling of being able to run as a wolf. The ability to move quickly and easily. She led him around the creek and returned to the woods. This was her home. Mike would be able to follow, but he didn't know the area like she did. That gave her an advantage.

He stayed right at her side the entire time. He could have easily overtaken her but seemed content to let her lead the way. She took a winding, curved route through the territory, running until she tired herself out. Only when she couldn't keep up the same pace did she slow and he did the same.

Spotting a good place to rest, she plopped down, panting. Mike curled around her and she relaxed against him. The heat from his body soaked into her tired bones. Becca didn't know why she hadn't thought about running before. It was the best way to relax and ease some of the recent stress. Maybe the entire Pack needed a night like this.

Becca was grateful that Mike had led her to this.

Closing her eyes, she managed to relax. His presence was a comfort to her. Instead of having to be alert and on watch she could let go for a few minutes. No one was there to look at her for answers.

As the Alpha's daughter, Becca was expected to be perfect at all times.

The pressure that was always present didn't normally bother her. Becca had been raised knowing what she could do to help the Pack. It wasn't always protection that they needed. Her position allowed her to care for people, to give them what they needed with a gentle touch. She didn't have to always be tough and strong like the Alpha. Becca was available to sit and talk with.

It could be exhausting.

But there were times and a few people who helped take the burden away.

She hadn't known that Mike would be one of them. How interesting that he'd given her exactly what she needed.

Becca didn't know how long they rested under the moon. She'd started to drift off when he nudged her shoulder. He rose trying to push her along. She moved to her four legs and started toward the creek. The trek back took more time as they moved slow still enjoying the peaceful night.

Once they made it to the spot where she'd left her clothes, he stopped and turned around again. She shifted to her human form and dressed. She picked up her camera before walking over to him then scratched his head again. He seemed to enjoy it, with his tail swishing back and forth and his tongue hanging out of his mouth.

She wasn't sure she'd ever met anyone who was as comfortable in the wolf form as Mike. It was nice.

Becca ended the scratching and patted his head then followed him as he started trotting toward the houses. Since they were headed in the direction of her own home, she suspected that he was escorting her.

The structure was almost in view by the time he veered off and she saw a pile of clothes. He stopped by them and glanced over at her.

"Oh, I suppose you want me to turn around since I made you?" she asked then gave an overly dramatic sigh as she did just that.

She heard movement behind her and barely resisted taking a peek.

"I actually wouldn't have minded at all if you'd watched," he said. "You've seen me naked before."

She turned, as he pulled his T-shirt down, disappointed that she only got a short glance at his muscular chest and small glimpse of the tattoo that covered it. She laughed. "Fair is fair, I guess."

He took a step toward her and she followed suit. "I have to say, I'm glad to see you again."

She tilted her head back to be able to look him in the eye. "Me, too. Although I wouldn't mind seeing even more of you. If you know what I mean."

They moved closer still. "Are you sure? I wouldn't want to overstep my welcome," he responded softly.

She could see the desire, the want that matched her own, reflecting back at her. She reached out and ran a palm over his chest. His hand covered hers.

"This might not be the best idea in the world," he admitted, giving her fingers a squeeze. "This is your home. I don't want to mess anything up for you."

She smiled and licked at her suddenly dry lips. "I guess there's one way to find out." Becca lifted onto her tiptoes and pressed her lips gently over his. He moaned before pushing back against her mouth harder.

Mike wrapped his arm around her waist as she opened for him and their tongues met. Oh, he tasted good. Spicy and unique. Becca remembered that flavor. She lifted her hands to dig into his shoulders as their kiss deepened and passion flowed between them.

Her head spun and she held on for dear life. Never had she been so turned on so fast. This was what she had been missing since their last encounter. This hunger that clawed at her.

He moved his hand over her body and she shuddered at his touch. Her pussy throbbed with need. She pulled him even closer, rubbed up and down, and hooked one leg up and over his hip.

He gripped her thigh, bucking against her body.

"Yes!" she hissed as their lips came apart and he continued to mouth down her neck.

"We should probably stop...slow down. Oh, God!" he murmured against her skin as she cupped his erection.

"Can't stop!" she answered, rocking against him. "Need you."

"Shit!" He pulled away and looked around. "There is no way in hell I want to stop."

He grasped her hand and yanked her against a large tree trunk that would offer them a little more privacy. She attacked the button and zipper of his pants. They pulled and tugged at clothing until they were both naked. Then he took her hand, urging her to the ground.

Becca lay on her back, not able to take her eyes off him as he lowered himself over her. Their lips met once again, this time slower and with more control. She arched into his touch as he ran his hands down her sides, opened for him while he settled his hips between her legs.

He kissed and ran his tongue down her neck, across her shoulder, then stopped to tease one of her nipples.

She gasped as Mike sucked and toyed with her.

"Such a beautiful body," he praised, moving to give the same attention to her other breast. "I've dreamed about this."

Becca pressed her legs against him and tilted her hips, trying to get pressure where she needed it. So had she. Becca needed Mike inside her again. She couldn't wait any longer.

He chuckled and moved lower, dipping his tongue into her belly button.

"Please," she begged and bucked up again.

Finally, after what seemed like hours, he pushed her legs open and rubbed his nose over her wet mound, breathing deep.

"Can't wait to taste you," he stated, and taste he did.

Becca cried out as he sucked and tongued her pussy. He teased her clit with his thumb while licking between her folds with his tongue. That wonderful tension began to build and she gasped as the tingle started to grow. She rode his face and moaned as he brought her over the edge of pleasure, clawing the moist dirt while she broke apart under the sexual assault.

Mike slid up her body before nipping her chin. Becca opened her eyes and saw his need. She reached down and gripped his hips. "Inside, come inside me."

He dropped soft kisses over her face. "I want to mark you. If I do, everyone will smell me on you. Are you okay with that?"

She puffed out a breath. "Yes, hurry."

He caught her chin between his finger and thumb. She looked at him, surprised. "I don't want you to regret this. Are you sure? Tell me now."

She nodded, lost in his dark gaze. His erection pressed against her flesh. Knew he wanted to take her like she was inviting him to.

"Mike, I want you." She gave him the words he seemed to need. "I don't care who knows about us."

He dropped his head and took a breath. "Thank God," he whispered.

Then he moved. Kissing her, thrusting his tongue inside her mouth while he lifted her hips and plunged inside her body.

She screamed in delight as his hard cock went deep.

Mike dropped his mouth down to her neck, sucking. The mark that he wanted to put on her. It wasn't a full mating. They were nowhere near that kind of commitment, but she could deal with her friends and family knowing that they'd been together.

She was proud to have Mike's interest.

Becca pressed her flesh harder against him. She was going to accept whatever Mike was willing to give her. She needed it.

Mike pulled out before sliding back in. She planted her feet on the ground and met him in one frenzied thrust after another. Sweat dropped from his forehead and landed on her chest and he continued to drive himself hard inside her. It was crazy and fast and awesome. She scratched her nails over his back as she climaxed once again.

He plunged a couple more times before throwing his head back and growling while he came. She wrapped her arms around his neck as he collapsed down onto her, their breathing fast and labored as they lay there wrapped around each other.

She'd been marked on the inside and out.

"Wow," she managed. "That was as good as the first time."

"Better," he said. Mike ran his hand down her back. "So much better."

Becca could live with that.

Chapter Three

Mike was still feeling light and happy as he showered and dressed for the day. After his encounter with Becca, he was settled for the first time since he'd left the service. Once they'd exhausted each other out in the woods, he'd walked her back to her home, the cottage he had passed on his way for his run. He had actually thought she would stay in the main house, but approved that the Alpha gave her both privacy and protection by providing her with her own space close by.

She explained about the apartment in town but had admitted to staying at the cottage more often than not.

He'd asked about the camera she had been carrying and they'd sat on the porch for over an hour while she'd told him about her career and he'd answered questions about his. He hadn't wanted to leave her, but she'd tried to hold back yawn after yawn. So he'd finally stood and kissed her deeply. He'd hated going back to his room alone but didn't think the Alpha would appreciate learning Mike had spent the night with his daughter. The subject would have to be broached eventually, though—Mike had given in to his need to leave his mark on her.

Mike hadn't been lying when he'd told Becca she wasn't like any other woman he'd ever met. She was beautiful, strong and fearless. Even after everything that she'd been through, last night she hadn't hesitated to get close to him as he'd lain there in his wolf form.

She had good instincts.

He stepped out of his room in jeans and a T-shirt and followed the scent and noise coming from the kitchen.

Kenny glanced up and grinned at him when he walked in. "Hey, man! You're just in time for the best breakfast. That is, if I don't eat it all before you get from the door to the table!" he said before shoving a huge bite of pancake into his mouth.

Mike smiled and accepted a cup of coffee from one of the women in the kitchen.

"Behave, Kenny, or I'll put you over my knee!" she said.

Kenny chuckled. "Yes, Mama."

Mike shook his head but took a seat next to him. The table was covered with dishes, the smells already hitting his stomach, causing his mouth to water. Eggs, sausage, bacon, pancakes, waffles and biscuits.

"Oh, man!" Mike picked up a plate and started to pile it with eggs. "I don't know when the last time was I saw so much food. Actually I do. This inn in New Mexico had the best food. And they served mainly shifters, so they knew how to pile it on."

"Wait until you see dinner," Kenny told him and stabbed his fork into one of the sausage links on the platter.

"I couldn't eat like this every day," Mike commented. "I'd weigh four hundred pounds."

Kenny snorted. A few more people came in and were introduced to him before Alpha Nelson joined them.

"Good morning, everyone," he greeted the group.

Mouths full, most responses were a nod. Kenny explained that anyone living or working at the main house were invited to every meal. The guards worked shifts so they would eat there at least once a day. It would give him time to meet who he was working with.

They were a friendly group. Only one of the younger men eyed him warily. Todd was seated next to Kenny and kept glancing at Mike. Once the women were done filling the platters and the stoves were turned off, they joined them, and Mike approved of the family atmosphere. He would have liked to have seen Becca there but guessed that since she had her own house, she probably didn't eat every meal at the main house.

"I would like to take Mike into town this morning. He mentioned he wanted to see the four spots of the fires," Kenny told Alpha Nelson when the man asked about their plans.

Mike nodded. "I've seen the pictures and while they were very good, I would like to get my own impressions."

"Yes." Alpha Nelson smiled. "Becca did a good job taking those. Although, it was hard on her seeing the places she'd grown up knowing, burned to the ground."

Mike hadn't thought about Becca being the one to photograph all the evidence. He hated that she'd had to do that. But she was indeed talented. No wonder her and Nikki had become such good friends. Mike didn't understand how either woman was able to look at something and bring it to life through a camera lens. It was artist.

"I want everyone here to give Mike what he needs. Full cooperation." The Alpha raised his eyes to meet each gaze of his Pack. "This ends soon."

Every head around the table bounced up and down at the order. Todd grumbled something under his breath, but even with Mike's superb hearing he didn't catch it. Kenny elbowed Todd and he grunted. Mike kept his face blank, pretending he hadn't noticed. Kenny seemed to be good friends with Todd, but Mike would still check him out.

Mike asked a few of the guys present who they thought might be involved in the fires and that opened the talk to a lot of speculation. He noted no one mention they thought it was someone in the Pack. All talk was about outsiders, not that that surprised Mike. No one wanted to believe a Pack member could be responsible. It would be the worst kind of betrayal.

When Alpha Nelson stood and said he had a few phone calls to make, Mike waited until he could catch Kenny's gaze. He motioned his head to the back.

"I think I'll take a walk," he said. "Just let me know when you're ready to go."

"Sure thing," Kenny replied. He eyed the man next to him. "There are a few things I need to take care of."

Mike took his time strolling around the property. He stayed away from the guest houses and kept close to the side of the Alpha house, appreciating the landscape and impressed with the way the grounds were taken care of.

He passed several young men who looked like they were heading into the main house. Mike nodded in greeting but didn't stop to talk.

When he reached the front of the house, he paused.

Becca was getting out of a black SUV. She had her phone up to her ear and was talking while waving her free hand around dramatically.

Mike watched, intrigued by the woman who had captured his attention so fast.

His breath caught when he saw Becca had noticed him, and smiled. She said something into the phone before taking it away from her ear and dropping it into her bag.

She sauntered up to him, grinning the entire time.

"Well, hello there, handsome," she greeted.

Mike couldn't help but smile down at her. "Becca."

He crowded into her personal space and was pleased when she didn't back away but instead pressed closer. She tilted her head and he caressed the side of her neck. Right over the bruise he'd left with his mouth. It felt hot, which turned him on.

"Good morning," he told her.

"Would have been better if I'd woken with you next to me," she said with a pout. "It was lonely waking all alone. No one to give me a proper start."

Mike leaned down a breath away. "I know." He didn't give her a chance to say anything more. Instead he pressed her lips down onto hers. She rose up and opened for him. He dived deep, stroking her tongue with his and locking their lips together. His cock hardened and pressed against the zipper of his jeans. Moaning into her mouth, he had to pull away before he took her down to the ground again.

Her face was flushed and she put a hand to her heart. "Jeez," she murmured.

Mike couldn't have said it better himself. Hell, he wasn't sure he could say anything.

"I stopped by to see my dad before I went into town but that kiss… Maybe I can be late."

He laughed. "I'm waiting on Kenny. We're heading into town ourselves. I want to look at the four sites."

She stepped back, frowning. "I still can't believe this. Or figure out why we were targeted. There are more important Packs than ours."

He raised an eyebrow, but slipped his arm around her shoulder. "We'll get to the bottom of it. But I think bringing in the tourists and having it known that this was the first community for shifters is the deciding factor."

"So this is our fault?"

"No," Mike said. "It actually gives a clue."

"How?"

"Whoever is doing this doesn't know the history or ranks of Packs. We were concerned this group would target the council. But if they're going after what the news is releasing, we can get ahead of them. If any of them slip through our fingers, we'll have an idea where they'll go next. We can make a plan."

Becca's shoulders relaxed. "That's the best news I've heard in weeks. I'd much rather go on the offense than stay on the defense."

"We will." Mike pulled her into a hug.

She let him hold her close for a few moments before she sighed. "I do need to be going. I'll see you tonight, then?"

Mike nodded. "Oh, you can count on that."

She smiled up at him, but it wasn't the one he was used to. This smile was more strained. "I hope you find something. We can't keep living like this. Wondering what will be next."

"It'll be okay," he assured her.

She kissed his cheek and stepped away. "I'd better go."

He watched her cut across the grass to open the front door. She glanced back one last time before disappearing inside. Mike was hard again and didn't want to meet up with Kenny in that state. He thought of every unsexy thing he could think of until his cock started to relax in his jeans.

He had some calls to make himself.

He dialed RJ first.

"Hello," RJ answered, out of breath.

"Bad time?" he asked, once again reminded how much RJ enjoyed his new mate.

RJ laughed. "I was running on the treadmill. Get your mind out of the gutter."

Mike chuckled. "Nikki's not home?"

RJ sighed. "No, she left this morning to go to Texas. She's doing an article on the recovery efforts from the hurricane."

No wonder RJ was working out. "Well, I hate to hear you have to do without your woman for a few days," Mike teased. "But I need your help."

"Thank God! I am so bored I was about to ask Ben and in if they needed help painting."

Mike snorted. "Manual labor?"

"Yeah."

"Okay, well, here's what I've got so far…"

RJ listened to everything before he sighed again. "I'll call Brandon and have him run the names."

"Okay."

"Then I'll call Casey and see if they have heard anything."

"That'd be good. For some reason, even with Zach being the Prince of the felines, he sure does know a lot about the wolf world."

RJ laughed and agreed. "I'll give you a call when I get something back."

"Tell Brandon to email me whatever he finds," Mike instructed.

"You got it, man. Take care."

Mike pressed the End button and thought about calling Nikki. He decided to wait until he had more time and privacy. He was certain Nikki would know what Mike could do to impress Becca. Her likes and needs. He was going to do more than have sex with her. Mike was going to court her. Old-fashioned, yes, but they had a real opportunity this time.

It had been his mistake not to get her phone number before. Mike would make up for that. He was free enough to come visit her. Plus, his parents requested his presence more and her Pack was on the way. There was a chance they'd make something work between them.

He might not be ready to settle down like his friends, but Becca was worth doing more than rolling around with.

The front door opened and Kenny jogged out. He spotted Mike and waved before motioning to one of the trucks parked close by. Mike swiftly made his way over to the vehicle. As soon as they were shut inside the vehicle, the obvious and strong scent of another wolf surrounded him. Kenny started the truck.

Before Mike could say anything, Kenny spoke. "I won't ask why you smell like Becca if you don't ask about Todd."

Mike shrugged. It was none of his business. Plus, Casey and Zach were together and had been for years and he loved both men. RJ's brother and Nikki's brother were also living together and very happy. It didn't bother him if Kenny and Todd had a relationship.

There was no question that Todd had marked Kenny with a 'keep away' warning to Mike. So, Todd was a little possessive. He couldn't find fault with that, either.

Mike chuckled. "I bet he feels better now."

Kenny barked out a laugh. "Yeah. Yeah, he does."

They didn't say anything else on the subject. Instead, Kenny filled Mike in on the town. They drove through the downtown district and Mike saw signs welcoming tourists and the bright, flashy décor. It was happy and inviting. They went farther until they got to a burned structure that had been taped off. The first stop was the community center, the site of the latest fire. As Kenny filled him in on what the center was used for, Mike studied the area. It had been a big chance to go after the center. It was only twelve blocks until they reached downtown where all the hotels and businesses were.

He and Kenny opened their doors and stepped out into the cool air. The smell of fire still hung heavy around them. Kenny told him what they'd found when he'd arrived as part of the fire station crew.

"You're a fireman, too?" Mike asked. That was impressive. He was beginning to like the guy. Not in a way to upset Todd. He had his hands full with Becca.

"Yeah." Kenny grinned. "I like my position for the Pack, but I love being a firefighter. It's what I always wanted."

Mike nodded. He moved closer to the building and investigated as well as possible. He would have preferred to be in his other form but that would have to wait until not so many people were around. Maybe he could come back at night. Or maybe someone already had?

"Anyone shift here?" he asked.

"Too risky," Kenny responded. "The tourists want to see a wolf, but our Alpha isn't going to put on a show for them. He says no one will get in trouble if we're caught in our other form, but we are not freaks. No one gets us to make us feel that way."

"The more I learn about the Alpha and Pack, the more I approve."

Kenny laughed. "I'm glad to hear you approve. I haven't traveled as much as you, but I understand how other Packs are run. I think things are about perfect here. Or they were before all these fires started happening."

"It'll be again," Mike promised.

Kenny glanced around nervously.

Mike tensed. "Something wrong?"

"Do you…do you think it might not be humans?"

"How do you mean?" Mike asked.

"The threatening letters are getting to my Alpha. What if it's another Pack trying to take over? Their leader might not be strong enough to challenge my Alpha so they're trying to run him off?"

"That's… That's actually a smart question," Mike praised. "I hadn't thought about it that way."

"It's one of the reasons that I'm worried about Becca. Everyone knows how much Becca means to our Alpha. If someone wants to hurt Alpha Nelson, Becca is the way to do it."

Mike growled. Kenny had a fucking point. "I can look into it."

"How?"

He grinned. "I know some pretty powerful people who owe me some favors. I'll figure this out. In the meantime, let's keep this discussion between us."

"Please." Kenny nodded. "I don't want to add any more worry to the Alpha if I'm wrong."

Mike wasn't sure of Kenny was right or wrong. It worried him, though. Another Pack would know exactly how to hurt the Alpha. Becca was in real danger. "Where's Becca now?"

"She's safe," Kenny said. "Todd is following her. He'll call if anything looks suspicious."

"Good, let's get this done then." He crouched down to study the area again. How the people responsible could have gotten in and an escape route. He could almost see it. "I'll come back tonight."

"Are you sure?"

"If it's safe. I'm good at sulking around."

"Okay," Kenny agreed. "Whatever you need."

He motioned for Kenny to follow him back to the truck to go to the other locations.

By the time Mike and Kenny had finished surveying all the sites, meeting with the arson investigators and police, and were seated at a booth at the local diner, Mike had a good idea that whoever was involved were not professionals.

Kenny shook his head when Mike shared that thought. "But how are they getting away with it then? No one ever saw them."

"They have to be getting help. I'm sorry, Kenny, but someone from the Pack has to be involved."

Kenny sighed and his shoulders slumped.

The waitress came by and refilled their coffee mugs. While she was at the table, Mike studied Kenny. He was attractive—tall, and, while not as broad and muscular as himself, he had a good, steady form. His blue eyes were a crystal-clear light color and his brown hair was a little long, so it curled around his ears and neck. He could see why Todd was attracted to him and why he'd wanted Mike to know.

But all Mike wanted was the dark-haired beauty he'd spent the night before with.

Kenny kicked his shin and Mike jerked and glared at him.

"I said we have company," he repeated.

Mike glanced over his shoulder and saw Todd walk in with Becca. She had her arm through Todd's and was laughing at something he said. Mike felt a growl rumble in his chest.

Kenny started to chuckle. "I see Todd's not the only jealous wolf in the room."

Mike kicked Kenny back but couldn't hide the smile that broke free. Kenny was right. Becca and Todd wove through the crowded restaurant until they were at the booth. Becca dropped down beside him and grinned.

"Funny running into you two here," she commented with a wink.

"Yeah, especially since I texted you and told you where we were," Kenny said with a raised eyebrow.

"Like Todd wouldn't have been able to find you anyway," Becca teased.

"I don't think we've formally been introduced," Mike said. "Mike Jackson."

Todd reached across the table and shook his hand. "Todd Wilkins."

Mike released his hand and put his arm around Becca's shoulders. She pressed close to him. Todd looked between the two of them several times. "Well, damn it."

And even Todd had to laugh with everyone else when he realized he didn't have any reason to be jealous.

Kenny patted his arm and kissed the side of his neck. "I told you, babe."

Todd waved the waitress over. "I hate you all," he said but was grinning ear to ear.

Dinner was good. The food—chicken-fried steak, mashed potatoes and coleslaw—reminded him of the bed and breakfast he stayed in while he'd visited friends in Coyote Bluff. He would have to go for a run tonight to work off breakfast and dinner. He couldn't keep eating like this. RJ always joked that they'd skipped so many meals while being out at some secret location that they should be able to eat whenever or whatever he wanted. But Mike had noticed that while RJ might say that, Nikki kept him eating healthier than RJ would let on.

That was what being mates was all about—taking care of one another.

Becca and Todd bantered across the table as Mike finally came up for air. He took a long drink of his coffee and leaned back. He was comfortable here. Settled. There were not very many places he felt he could relax, that didn't leave him feeling an itch between his shoulder blades that made him want to reach for the service pistol he no longer carried. He didn't want to lose the feeling either, so long he had searched for a way to feel comfortable in his own skin again.

When talk about the fire made the way into the conversation, he could sense the sadness coming from Becca. He ran his fingers through Becca's thick hair. She sighed and leaned in to his touch. Movement to the side drew his attention.

He looked over at one of the officers he'd met earlier in the day. The man smiled in passing.

Yeah, it was a pretty great community.

"You ready to get out of here?" Todd asked Kenny. "I need to stop by the firehouse and pick up a few things."

Kenny looked at Mike. "You done with me?"

Todd growled, which made Mike grin. He ran his thumb over the fading mark on Becca's throat. Damn shifter healing. It would be gone in a few more hours.

"I'll let you freshen it up," she whispered.

"Go." Mike waved at Kenny. "Go away."

Kenny laughed before pushing Todd out of the booth. Mike didn't take his gaze off Becca.

"We should all go."

"Yes," Becca agreed. "That sounds like a plan."

Becca shivered in the cool night air. She only had jeans and a T-shirt on. She'd forgotten the light jacket she normally carried when she'd left the house earlier that morning. Her mind had been on other things. Like getting to see Mike again.

Mike followed her to her SUV. "Cold?"

She glanced back at him. "Yes, but I think you can warm me up."

Becca laughed when he reached for her and she jumped away. She hit the Unlock button on the key she carried to the Tahoe and climbed in the driver's side as Mike opened the passenger door. They closed the doors and were quickly surrounded by darkness. She scooted to the edge of her seat, at the same time he reached for her. Their lips met and she moaned into his mouth. This was what she had been waiting for all day. What she had needed. Becca slipped her hands under the hem of Mike's shirt. His skin was hot and smooth.

He broke away, panting. "What I want to do to you can't take place in the parking lot of a diner," he informed her.

She laughed. "My apartment is only a couple blocks away."

"Well...what are you waiting for?" he asked.

She shook her head and with a trembling hand put the key in the ignition. She drove as carefully as she could. It wasn't easy with Mike's hand busy moving from her breasts to cup her pussy. Becca still had her clothes on, but she could swear she felt his touch burn her flesh.

"We're here." She pulled into her parking space at the edge of her staircase. The apartment was behind the bakery. A remodeled garage loft that had once been the owners' son's place and that they now rented out. She wasn't sure if she would renew her lease when it expired a few months down the road. Oh, she loved the little place, but she spent most of her time at her cottage. The cottage was home.

Becca yanked her seatbelt off and lunged for Mike. He met her halfway so they were in each other's arms once again. She needed him. Burned for him. It hadn't even been twenty-four hours and she wasn't sure how it had happened, but she had become addicted to Mike Jackson's kisses and touch.

"Inside," Mike whispered. "We need to get inside."

She tore herself away and nodded. "Come on." Becca led Mike up the stairs and unlocked the door. She pushed it open and grabbed Mike's hand, pulling him forward.

Once he was inside, she slammed the door closed and pushed him against it.

She attacked his mouth once again. He obviously wasn't complaining since he tightened his hands he had buried in her hair. Becca nipped his lower lip before she started to nibble her way down. He raised his arms and helped when she pushed his shirt off his chest.

She traced the tattoo over his left pectoral. It was a detailed tattoo with two wolves, a black puma, a bobcat and a hawk. "I saw this last time. You usually distract me before I can ask about it. What's it mean?" she asked running her fingers over the ink. "It's wonderful, so detailed and lifelike." She'd never seen such detail before.

"That's me and my brothers, the unit I was in," he managed.

Becca grinned—his mind wasn't on his tat. He had more pressing matters.

He hissed as she popped open his button and slid the zipper down. She reached into his boxers and pulled out his hard cock. He moaned and she dropped to her knees. She pushed and yanked his pants and boxers down his legs and removed his boots and socks.

Once she had him naked, she looked up at him. Mike was leaning back against the front door, his head down as he stared at her.

She gripped his erection and jacked him a few times. He moved his hips.

"Please, baby, please."

She loved the begging. She bent her head and licked at the moisture escaping from his slit.

He hissed fisting his hands at his side.

She kissed and licked some more before sliding her mouth down his hardness.

Mike gripped her head, although he didn't direct her in any way, held on as she moved her mouth over him. He pumped gently into her mouth, but she didn't want gentle. She wanted to feel him lose control.

Using her hand and tongue, she increased the suction. She enjoyed the hardness against her tongue, the salty essence she got small tastes of. With her free hand, she caressed his muscular thigh. He shook under her touch.

"Good, so good, baby," he murmured, thrusting harder.

She encouraged him with a hum and he started to rock into her faster.

It wasn't long before he was grunting and gripping her hair harder. "Gonna…"

He was warning her. She could let off now if she wanted. She didn't want to, though. She hummed again and he stiffened before releasing into her waiting mouth. She relaxed her throat to take all of him that she could.

She gave his cock a few more licks before pulling away and sitting back on her heels.

"God, you're beautiful," he praised and reached for her.

He helped her stand before his lips closed over hers. She opened her mouth and he swept his tongue inside and tasted himself. When he bent down and lifted her, she wrapped her legs around his waist and held onto his shoulders.

"Bedroom?" he asked.

"Right behind you," she told him.

He carried her into the dark cool room and closed the door behind them. Mike undressed her slowly, taking time to kiss and caress every inch of her skin. By the time she was naked and they'd fallen onto the soft mattress, she was more than ready for him. He covered her with his body, sucking on her neck. The same spot that he'd concentrated on the previous night. That seemed to be a thing, marking her. Becca hoped it was something that he always wanted to do. She'd wear it proudly.

Becca bucked up against him.

He chuckled into her skin. "Impatient."

She moaned. "Don't tease."

As he ran his hands over her body, learning and caressing, she hummed in approval. She wasn't thin but didn't consider herself overweight, either. She was a happy size fourteen and proud of her body. Mike seemed to appreciate her curves just fine.

When she couldn't stand it anymore, Mike finally trailed his fingers down her stomach to her pussy. She was wet for him and his digits slid inside easily.

She rode two fingers as he pumped them. As good as it felt, it wasn't enough. "Mike…"

"Yes, baby," he said and finally…finally pushed her legs wide and positioned himself.

He plunged inside and Becca arched. "Yes…yes."

"Yes," he repeated. He rode her hard, grasping her hips as he thrust deep.

Skin slapping against skin echoed around the room. She met each and every frenzied move. It was wild and hard and what she wanted. This was what being with another shifter meant. Mike could be as rough as he wanted and all Becca could do was demand more.

As good as it was, she couldn't help but grasp at the peak of completion. "Mike, I need — "

He pulled out, making her cry with the denial. No, no, no. Becca tried to grab at him, but he flipped her over onto her hands and knees.

"I'll give you what you need," he said. With a low, long growl, he plunged back in.

Becca shouted as pleasure swamped her. Several more hard thrusts and she was calling his name into the dark room.

Her body milked his cock. She made sure to tighten every muscle she could control.

He grunted then threw his head back. One last time, Mike buried himself deep and let go.

Warm seed filled her and she sighed. Her arms were trembling, so she let herself drop down. Marked again. This was becoming a habit. One she hoped continued.

They lay there for several long minutes, Mike's heavy body pressing her into the mattress. It felt right. He brushed the hair off the back of her neck with a gentle hand before kissing her flesh. His lips were warm. She was hot.

She was also confused. This was more than another roll between the sheets. Now she knew who Mike was, Becca was going to have to deal with feelings that she wasn't ready for. She didn't think Mike would be, either. Except Becca couldn't watch him walk away again. Or had it been her? One of them had.

There was so much they needed to talk about. Becca didn't want Mike to learn about her past from anyone else but her. She wasn't looking for a mate. Men got nervous when they thought a female was.

Becca wasn't in love. The word *yet* bounced around her head, though. She'd been in love once before. At least that was what she had thought it was at the time. And she'd almost let the pressure from family and friends, the Pack, push her into a mating ceremony.

Kurt had stopped the madness before it had gotten that far. Although it had broken her heart when he'd left her, she understood now why he'd had to go.

If he hadn't, she wouldn't have had this chance with Mike—this big, scary, exciting chance.

Becca rolled onto her back when Mike moved off her. She glanced up into his warm eyes. He was so handsome.

Mike dropped his forehead against hers and breathed.

Becca smiled. This was something she was glad she hadn't missed.

Mike peppered kisses across her nose and cheeks before groaning as he lifted himself up.

"Shower?" he inquired.

She waved in the direction of the bathroom.

"Tired?"

"Comfy," she corrected, hugging the pillow to her. "Hurry and come back to bed."

The bed shifted as he stood. Becca turned back to bury her face into the pillow. She was almost asleep when Mike's weight was back on top of her.

She wiggled her ass under him and felt him start to respond. He cupped her hips.

"None of that," he said, bending to kiss the back of her neck. "Time for sleep."

"'Kay," she mumbled, already sinking again.

He laughed and moved off to her side. She picked up the sheet and let him slip underneath. When he pulled her close, she settled against him. He made a better pillow, anyway.

She laid her head on his chest and wrapped an arm around his waist, content and happy.

Chapter Four

The shrill sound of a cell phone woke Mike and Becca's quiet voice answered, but it was the caller who woke him completely. He could hear the frantic voice through the line. The lamp beside the bed switched on and Becca sat up.

"Todd, slow down," Becca snapped. "What are you talking about?"

Mike could make out Todd's response. "Where are you? Your car's not in front of the cottage! Where are you! Are you okay?"

"Todd!" Becca shouted. She glanced over at Mike with a frown. "I'm fine. We're at my apartment."

"Oh, God! Oh, thank God! I was so scared!"

"Todd, what is going on?" Becca asked.

Mike ran a hand down her back. The call was upsetting her.

There was a pause then another voice on the line.

"Becca? You're at your apartment?" Kenny asked.

"Yes! Now what is happening?"

"I'm sorry, honey, but your cottage was torched."

"My...my house?" she cried and jumped from the bed. The sheet fell away as she scrambled for her jeans.

"Yes. I'm sorry. Is Mike there with you?"

"Ye-yes." She looked over at him and he saw the tears gathering in her eyes. "My house?" she asked again.

"Yes, sweetie. I need you to remain calm. Between Todd and your dad, we already have our hands full. Can I talk to Mike?"

She held the phone out to him. Mike moved, since she seemed frozen.

He brushed her hair out of her eyes and pressed a gentle kiss to her lips. "It will be okay, baby," he told her. He waited for her nod before he took the phone. "Kenny?"

Kenny and Mike only spoke briefly. Mike promised to bring Becca back as soon as possible. She hadn't moved. She still stood in the middle of the room, gripping her jeans. She hadn't even dressed. He disconnected the phone and wrapped his arms around her, holding her close.

"My house?" Her voice shook and sounded far away.

He kissed her again. "I'll get these guys. I swear I will, honey."

She nodded. It was his job to protect her. He'd failed her by letting this affect her so deeply, but he had to push back that anger. He'd catch these bastards. That would be a promise that he could keep. "Let's get dressed. We'll check out the damage."

"Another building down," Becca said. "This time inside Pack territory."

"Remember they want to make you suffer," Mike said.

"They succeeded."

Crissy Smith

"No," Mike stated. "They might have hurt you a little, but they aren't going to destroy you."

"Okay, I can do this. We need to hurry."

They dressed quickly, not speaking again. Her hands shook a little, but Becca held herself together pretty well. Mike took her hand to lead her down the stairs. What a difference a few hours made. When they'd arrived at the small apartment, they'd been blissful and horny. Now, he was leading a heartbroken Becca down to her vehicle and he wanted to strangle someone.

The drive back to the Pack property took no time at all. Becca remained quiet, staring out of the passenger window. There were more cars around than Mike could remember seeing since he'd arrived.

Becca sighed and turned to him. Instead of tears, he saw anger. "We're going to end these attacks on the Pack. This ends. No one else is going to lose what they love."

Mike nodded. "Yes." Good, Becca's strength would be able to help her deal with whatever they arrived at.

She surprised him by leaning over and grabbing his face. She kissed him hard. "And make them pay for ruining the most wonderful night."

Mike smiled. "You got it."

She reached for the door handle, pausing to take a deep breath, then climbed out of the SUV. Mike hurried to follow. Instead of going to the main house, she walked around the large structure following the path to her house. Mike stayed by her side for the short walk.

Ahead of them, he could see the Alpha, several guards, Todd, Kenny and Eric.

Todd broke away from the group and jogged toward them. He threw himself at Becca.

"I'm so sorry! I was so scared."

Becca laughed and patted his back. "It's okay. I understand." Mike felt better when she released Todd and shifted closer to him. Mike squeezed her shoulder.

"How bad is it?" she asked.

Todd averted his gaze. "Come on. Let's get this over with."

Mike and Becca followed behind Todd toward the crowd. When Becca reached her dad, he opened his arms allowing her to bury her face into his chest.

It wasn't until he sniffed her and glanced over at him with a look close to shock that Mike remembered that she hadn't showered yet. But whatever Alpha Nelson was thinking, he didn't show it. He rocked his daughter and told her how they would build bigger and better.

She pushed away finally. "Okay, let me see it."

Alpha Nelson placed an arm around her shoulder and slowly walked closer to the cottage. It was still standing, unlike the community center. But the fire was evident. The beautiful front porch was gone and the left side of the house still had water dripping from the exposed beams.

Becca gasped.

Mike wanted to comfort her, but her dad was already there. "At least you weren't here," Alpha Nelson told her.

The scene didn't look like any of the others. Something bugged him about the entire setup. Why would they have gone after her cottage and not the main house? Someone had taken the trouble to get onto Pack territory but hadn't targeted the Alpha. Mike avoided looking at anyone else as he moved closer and tried to pick up any differences between the first four fires and this one. He motioned to Kenny and stepped back away from the group. Kenny and Todd followed.

"I want to shift," Mike told them.

Kenny nodded. "Okay, I'll tell Alpha Nelson and see if he can take Becca and everyone else into the main house. Todd, go with him."

Todd looked between Becca and him. Mike had a feeling he wasn't happy at letting Becca out of his sight so soon.

"The best way to help her is to find who is responsible," Mike announced.

Todd sighed but nodded and waved him over. "Okay."

They moved away from the others and both scented around to make sure they were alone. Todd turned his back and Mike shed his clothing then started his shift.

Once in his other form, he shook then butted his head against Todd's side.

Todd reached down and patted his head. "Okay, Fido, let's go."

Mike growled at the dog name, but Todd laughed. By the time they'd made their way back to the cottage, only Kenny and Becca remained.

Mike trotted over to Becca. She dropped down and grabbed his head. "Thank you."

He licked her face, making her laugh. She let him go and he looked over at Kenny.

Kenny shrugged. "Like you could have gotten rid of her, either."

Mike huffed at him.

Becca patted his head, then smacked Kenny's arm before waving toward her ruined house. "Well, have at it."

Mike blocked everything out but the house and the scents surrounding it. Burning wood was the strongest, but he did his best to ignore that. He could now smell the gas that had been used on it. He separated the scents of the others. Some he knew and a few he didn't.

He climbed and hopped over the mess and the part that had fallen. He sniffed and scented, taking his time, wanting to do right by Becca.

When he'd finally gathered all the information he could, he made his way back over to the other three. She raised an eyebrow, but he merely shook his head. Then nodded over to his clothes.

"I'll come with you," Becca said.

"I don't think he needs help dressing," Kenny teased.

"I'm supervising," she called over her shoulder, following him when he trotted back to his clothes. She didn't turn around but watched him shift and dress.

As soon as he pulled his shirt over his head, he felt her arms around his waist.

He hugged her close. Her body was cold and he ran his hands briskly over her arms. "Let's get you inside."

"I'm okay," she said.

"That's going to have to wait, anyway," Kenny said, coming into view.

Mike glanced at him.

"There's someone who wants to talk to you two."

Kenny wouldn't say anything more, led Mike and Becca into the dense woods they had run in the night before.

Mike held Becca's hand while they stepped over a fallen log. He didn't like heading into the unknown, but Becca hadn't argued. He kept an eye on Kenny and Todd in front of them. The two men didn't walk close at all. There was more distance between them than Mike had ever seen.

That gave him even more reason to be uncomfortable.

Becca squeezed his hand. Mike tried to smile for her. No matter what, he would protect her. Even if he didn't know where the threat might come from.

They were close to the creek before Mike finally got the scent of other shifters. Not all wolves, either. Becca stiffened and he pulled her closer. She shook her head, though.

"Kenny!" she whispered quietly. "You're kidding me!"

Kenny looked over his shoulder. "Sorry."

Mike didn't know what was going on but more and more he found he didn't like it. The hairs on the back of his neck stood up. He spread his legs to brace for an attack.

"He wants to talk to you and meet Mike."

Mike looked down at Becca. Her jaw was clenched. "What's going on?"

Becca snorted. "Everything's okay. I'm going to kill Kenny later."

They reached the water where two men waited. One stepped away and walked toward them. Becca paused and, still holding his hand, let the other two meet with the stranger. The stranger stopped at Kenny and pulled him into his arms.

Mike expected Todd to react. But he didn't. Once the man had released Kenny with several slaps on his back, he shook Todd's hand.

Kenny glanced in their direction. Mike didn't know what look he sent Becca, but it didn't help calm him any. The Pack knew this man, but the reception was odd.

The man stepped toward them. Mike could see the resemblance between him and Kenny now. The stranger was bigger than Kenny but had the same brown hair and crystal-blue eyes. His hair was shaved and he screamed military.

Mike would guess it was Kenny's older brother.

The stranger smiled at them, his gaze lingering on their joined hands.

"Hey, Becca," he greeted.

She nodded. "Kurt."

The stranger looked at him. "Kurt Moore. I've heard a lot of good things about you, Mike," he said, holding out his hand.

He had to drop Becca's hand to take it. He didn't like that, but he didn't want to be rude, either. There was a certain protocol when dealing with Packs.

"Thank you. I'm sorry, but I can't repeat the compliment yet."

Kurt nodded. "I spoke to Prince Zachary and his mate Casey yesterday. Casey assured me you would be able to help take down whoever was after the Pack."

He shouldn't have been surprised. It seemed the feline Prince knew everything and everyone. Casey, who had been his unit's leader, was as bad.

"Well, I have yet to fail and there's no way this will be the first time," Mike assured him. He didn't know why but he had the strongest urge to pull Becca into his arms. To claim her before the stranger. He barely resisted. "Kenny said you wanted to speak with us?"

Kurt nodded and spoke to Becca. "I'm sorry about your cottage. I know how much you loved that place."

"Thank you," Becca responded.

"We were following a lead. Clint"—he motioned back to his man—"caught a scent that didn't belong after the last fire. We found several human males staying in a cabin about fifteen miles out of town."

"Are they involved?" Mike asked.

Kurt shook his head. "We don't know, but we believe so. We overheard several conversations about getting rid of the 'unnatural creatures' but they were still at the cabin at the time of the fire here."

"They could be working with someone else," Mike offered.

"Someone in the Pack," Kurt finished.

"Do you know who?" Becca inquired.

"I have it narrowed down to three people. I left two men watching the humans. They'll call us if they move. But I wanted to see the fire myself. I asked Kenny to let me tell you." He said the last part to Becca.

Mike didn't like this at all. But he was pretty sure he had it figured out.

Becca shrugged. "It's fine with me."

"Who's on the short list from the Pack?" Mike probed.

"Shawn Cross, Fred Withermore and Owen Nobles."

"Owen Nobles? The officer working the case?" Mike asked. He was already checking out the other two men who Kenny had thought of.

Kurt nodded. "What better cover? Plus he was at the main house tonight and he knows you're looking into the fires. Add in your...relationship with Becca and I think that's why he went after her. To send a message."

Mike was watching Becca. Her eyes narrowed in annoyance.

"That's not *anyone's* business," Becca snapped. The emphasis on anyone was not lost on Mike or Kurt, for that matter.

Kurt held up his hands. "Becca—"

She waved her hand in the air. "Whatever, go on."

"We'll continue to watch the humans if you'll keep an eye on the other three. We don't want to get too close.

Alpha Nelson and Kenny knew we were here, but no one else did. I think it's best we keep it that way."

"My dad knew?" Becca asked.

Kurt stepped toward her. "It's complicated."

She backed up and turned on her heel. "It always is. If you'll excuse me, it's cold out here and I'm going back to the main house."

Becca stomped off toward the Alpha house. Mike let her get out of earshot before he turned on Kurt. "What are you saying?" There'd been plenty of information Kurt had shared, but he could read people well.

Kurt stared after Becca. "They could have killed her," he whispered.

"She wasn't here."

"I know." He blew out a breath. "She'd more important to the Pack than most people know. It's Owen. I can feel it in my bones."

"He'll be watched," Mike said.

"The way these humans were talking at the cabin, they don't care who they hurt. This isn't a random group of crazies. They are a real threat."

"I'll do what I can," Mike promised. "I'll let Kenny know what I find and if I need to get with you."

Kurt sighed. "Thanks." He trailed off and looked after Becca. "Watch her. There's no telling what she'll do," Kurt requested.

Mike bristled. Becca was his to worry about. He had a pretty good idea she and Kurt had been involved at one time but now Mike was in the picture. He wasn't going to step aside. Not unless Becca told him to.

"I've got her. Don't worry about that."

Kurt turned away. "Yeah," he muttered. "I hope so."

Mike didn't say anything else, jogged after Becca. He caught up with her long, angry strides but didn't comment. Didn't ask the questions he was dying to get answers to.

Becca strode into the house through the patio doorway. Alpha Nelson and his Beta, Eric, were standing inside the living room.

Alpha Nelson hurried to his daughter. "It was best you didn't know."

Becca shook her head. "That wasn't a decision you should have made for me. And I can't believe you did."

"Becca…"

She stepped away. "I'll be upstairs."

Mike wasn't sure whether to follow or not. Alpha Nelson made the decision for him by placing his hand on Mike's shoulder.

"She'll be okay once she calms down. She sees this as a kind of betrayal. From me and Kenny. Her anger is covering her shock. I know the way my daughter thinks."

Mike didn't comment, just nodded. He could see Becca's point of view, but he was unsure where it left them.

"Give her time to get over the shock and she'll prove how remarkable she really is," he added.

"I can already tell," Mike confessed.

Alpha Nelson locked gazes with him and smiled. "Yes, I believe you can."

With that said, the Alpha patted his back and Mike was dismissed. He wasn't sure where Becca had gone or if she even wanted to be found. Maybe she needed time, like her father had said.

He climbed the stairs to his room. He had some calls he could make. And maybe he needed to make the one to Nikki. She might be able to give him some history on Becca and Kurt Moore. He opened the bedroom door and stopped short. Becca stood at the window, staring out at the darkness. He was relieved she had gone to his room. That said something about her feelings, didn't it?

"You okay?" he asked, closing the door.

She sighed. "It was so unexpected, you know. The fire, seeing Kurt…"

He didn't like the softness in her tone when she'd said his name.

She turned and he realized he was growling. She lifted an eyebrow. "I guess I should explain."

Mike shrugged. "Only if you want." That lie barely came off his tongue.

Becca laughed. "Really? So you're not wondering what happened between him and me? You'll wait until I feel like telling you?"

She was challenging him, and while he respected that in the woman, his wolf scratched in dominance. To prove and fight for his female. Mike gave in to the wolf side.

"No. I don't want to know what happened. I don't want to hear if you were in love with him, or if it was sex, or why it didn't work out. I want you to tell me he doesn't matter."

She pressed her lips together and Mike regretted his outburst. It wasn't his place to demand anything.

"Well, you get to hear it all," she told him. "You get to know whether you want to or not because I won't let this push us apart."

"Us?" he probed. "So there is still an us?"

She smiled. For the first time since she'd found out about the fire, she looked at him with the same passion as earlier. "You won't get rid of me that easily."

Mike sat on the bed. "Then what are you doing way over there?"

He chuckled as she launched herself from the window to him. He caught her weight easily and wrestled her under him.

"If you're going to tell me about an ex, I want to be able to touch you. To make sure you know it's my hands on you, not his," Mike confessed.

She reached up and cupped his face. "I know who I'm with, Mike Jackson."

He bent and kissed her gently, holding himself in check so as not to get carried away. Mike pulled back. "Tell me about him," he requested.

Becca pushed on his chest and he sat back up. She scooted close to him, though, sitting cross-legged in front of him, her legs over his, which made both the human and wolf sides happy.

"I started to date Kurt before I graduated high school. He was older, and at first my dad didn't like it, but Kurt promised my dad that nothing physical would happen as long as I was underage. He kept that promise."

She looked up at him as if gauging his reaction. He gave her a small smile. It was all he could manage.

"I was still in school when he went into the service. The plan was he'd do his time while I finished high school and started college. He came back whenever he had leave. Everything was going okay." She started to play with the edge of the comforter. "Then it changed."

Mike sat silent, waiting for her to finish.

"He was supposed to be getting out and would become the head of security for the Pack. I was planning our mating ceremony."

Mike sucked in a breath. He hadn't even considered their relationship had got that far.

"He surprised me by coming home one weekend. I was excited, thought he was home for good. That's when he told me he'd re-enlisted. That he wasn't going to mate me."

Mike dropped his head. Did that mean she still loved Kurt?

"I was devastated," she told him. "Everyone was. It was supposed to be the perfect match for the Pack. And instead Kenny had to put his fire training on hold and I was alone. Tonight was the first time I've seen Kurt since."

Mike was afraid to ask but he had to. "Do you still love him?"

Becca laughed, a small but happy sound. "I will always love Kurt. He was my first love, you know." She reached for his hands. "But I am not in love with him. I don't think I was even in love with him when I was planning our ceremony."

Mike frowned. Now he was even more confused.

"Kurt was never cruel to me. You should know that. After we spoke he offered to give it more time, to keep dating and hold off on the ceremony. To give me time to grow up. He could remain in the military, do one more tour, before coming back to mate with me and take the position with the Pack...if I could tell him I loved him more than anything in the world, and was ready to settle down for the rest of my life. That there was nothing and no one else I wanted. That I was okay with my life always remaining the same."

She took a deep breath. "And I couldn't do it. Faced with having him in front of me and asking for the first time what I wanted. No one had ever asked me that, not even my dad. Everyone had assumed I wanted to mate and have us start our lives together. But I couldn't do it. And Kurt had known.

"He made the hard decisions for me that night. Made himself the bad guy. I blamed him for a long time. For years, I hated him, even if I knew deep down we'd been rushing into a commitment."

"What changed?" Mike inquired.

"I did. I finished college and went on my first assignment away from home. I traveled for another month. Took my pictures and met good friends. I would have never have been able to do that. Not then. I thought about writing to him a few years ago to see if I could repair our friendship because above all else we had been friends. Kenny didn't know how to get hold of him and I couldn't ask my dad. I was worried he'd think there was a chance of us getting back together." She pulled him closer. "I like my life. I am very happy. I wasn't meant to be with Kurt. I know that and he knows that. I want more now."

"What do you want?" he whispered and leaned toward her.

"I want everything. I want it all. My happily ever after. I deserve that. I was upset because my dad and Kenny kept something big from me. But I was scared that you would see Kurt and question what I felt for you."

"Me?" he teased. "Worried about me?"

She grinned. "Yes. You are who I want, Mr. Jackson. Already what I feel is strong. And this time, I get to be myself. There's no pressure or expectations. I want to explore what is happening between us. I want to see where we can end up."

Pressing his mouth over Becca's, he swallowed the sound when she moaned. He could work with that. Hell, he felt the same way.

"Tell me you feel the same," she pleaded.

"I do," he told her. "You're mine." He moved his mouth to her neck, nibbling and sucking.

"Marking me?" she asked running her hands under his shirt. "Again."

Mike sucked harder before propping himself up on his elbows. "That's to start."

"Yes," she agreed. "A good start."

Mike laid her on the bed towering over her. "Now how about I get my scent all over you? Wouldn't want anyone to think you're available."

"That's a trick Todd uses a lot," Becca commented.

"Where did you think I got it from?" he quipped.

She laughed, filling the room with the sound of her delight.

* * * *

Becca woke wrapped around Mike's solid form, her head on his shoulder and their hands clasped over his chest. She felt lighter after her talk with Mike the night before. Her confession to Mike had opened old wounds, but she was glad to have gotten it out of the way.

She was upset with her dad and her best friend, but she knew why they had kept Kurt's appearance a secret. And after thinking about it, she was glad they had. There was no way of knowing how she would have reacted to the knowledge that her ex was close by. Becca hadn't lied when she'd told Mike she wasn't in love with Kurt. It had taken a lot of years for her to realize that their relationship was what everyone else had wanted. She'd gone along with it for no other reason than it had been expected.

The Pack had wanted the connection. Wanted a strong mate for her in case something happened to the Alpha. She would never regret her time with Kurt. And even better, she could look back at that time with fond memories, but that was all they would ever be — memories. She had a life without him. She was happy.

She crawled out of bed without disturbing Mike. She had to look down at him one more time. Mike was handsome, strong and kind — the kind of man she had pictured she would end up with. Not that she was in a hurry to mate. It would be a long time before she went down that road again. But she would like to spend time with Mike, to start to make new memories. She wanted Mike in her life.

The morning before — and God, did that seem like years ago now — she'd contacted her friend Nikki to get all the dirt on Mike.

They'd exchanged text messages, each one of Nikki's consisting of her singing Mike's praises. It had been obvious to Becca that Nikki wanted to play matchmaker. Becca took a lot of enjoyment in informing her that she didn't need the help.

Nikki was pleased. Happy for her.

She'd met Nikki on one of her very first assignments away from home. Nikki had been writing an article on endangered red wolves in the United States. Becca had been asked to accompany her to take the photos.

Once they had realized they shared the shifter gene, they had become fast friends.

Becca knew that Nikki still took assignments all over even though she had mated. That was the way Nikki was. She liked what she did. Becca preferred to be home. It was one of the few things they didn't have in common.

Of course, the last time Becca had taken a job out of the country was before her friend had her mating ceremony. Becca had made it back just in time. Otherwise she'd have missed out on meeting Mike. Now Mike was there in her town Becca really wanted to believe there was some sort of connection that was meant to be. Maybe not fate, but something along those lines? Perhaps. Becca didn't want to think about what would happen if she'd never met Mike at all.

It really was a small world when a person thought about it — the connections that drew people together.

The connection that helped to keep the shifter communities thriving even with the threats coming at them now.

Becca pulled jeans and a T-shirt out of her drawers and hurried to the shower. There was something she wanted to do first before she dealt with anything else.

She took a quick shower and dressed then managed to get out of the bedroom and downstairs without running into anyone. Becca avoided the kitchen, knowing that was where most people would be, slipped out of the door in the den and quickly made her way toward the woods. She wasn't quiet once outside in order to let anyone out know she was coming. If Kurt and his friends were staying in the area, she knew where to find him.

She passed the creek and went farther north. Before she got to the old hangout, she heard movement.

Kurt walked toward her and she paused to let him finish closing the distance. He smiled at her but nervously shoved his hands in his jeans. He wasn't wearing a shirt or shoes.

He was more attractive now he'd aged, with tan firm skin and a muscular body. But she was also relieved when she didn't feel the same stirring inside at the sight of him half naked. She was truly over him.

"Hey, Becca," he greeted.

She nodded. "You got a minute to talk?"

He motioned toward a pile of rocks they could sit on. She led the way and took a seat. Once he was beside her, she turned to face her old friend.

"I'm sorry, Becca. I should have told you I was back. That I was helping," he started.

She held up a hand to stop him. "No, Kurt. You've apologized enough. It's my turn."

He jerked back. "What? No."

"Yes," she sighed. This was harder than she thought. "I was mad at you for a long time. I blamed you for leaving me."

"I did," he interrupted.

"No," she corrected. "I let you go. You were right that night when you asked if I was one hundred percent sure I was ready to settle down for the rest of my life. If I felt it in my bones that we were meant to be together forever. You knew."

His shoulders slumped. "I only ever wanted what was best for you."

"I know that." She laughed. "Well, I know that now anyway." She looked at him—really looked at her ex-lover and friend. He'd changed, but remained the same honest man. He had laugh lines around his eyes. The blue color still sparkled. Even with several days of not shaving and staying out in the woods, he looked great. But he wasn't what she wanted anymore.

"It took a lot of guts to come to me and end things. To follow your path and not give in to what everyone else thought was best. I'll always be grateful to you for being able to do that."

Kurt rubbed his hands over his knees. "Is this where you tell me you don't love me anymore? That you're happy with Mike?" he asked.

Becca reached for one of his hands. She threaded her fingers through his. "No, I'll always love you. That won't change. I told Mike the same last night. And as far as what I feel about Mike?" She shrugged. "I don't know where that will go. I enjoy him. Like being with him. But it's new and right in the middle of the most difficult thing I've ever faced. Only time will tell. But I'm glad I have the chance to see what will happen."

Kurt cupped her cheek with his free hand. "Tell me you're happy."

Becca turned her head and kissed his wrist. "I am. I really am. And I think you are too. But I want you to do something for me."

Kurt dropped his hand and nodded. "Anything."

"Stop staying away. After this is over, come home every once in a while. Your brother misses you, the Pack misses you and I miss you."

"You mean that?" he asked. "I don't want to upset you."

"Kurt, I never wanted you to stay away. This is your Pack, too. You belong here. When you're ready, I want you to visit. I want to be friends. Real friends."

Kurt squeezed her hand. "I want that, too."

Chapter Five

Mike stepped out of the kitchen door into the bright morning sun. Becca walked out of the coverage of the trees and he smiled. He had opened his eyes that morning in hopes of continuing where they had left off the night before when they had collapsed, spent and tired. But he'd woken alone.

He'd hid his disappointment at her disappearance while he enjoyed his breakfast of fresh baked bread, eggs and ham with some of the others in the house. While eating, he'd received the news that no one had been able to find Owen. Owen hadn't been seen since before the fire last night. The guy was looking guilty now. Everyone involved with the Pack should be around when the daughter of the Alpha's house burned down. Especially someone involved in the case.

Mike had left a message for Brandon at the sheriff's office back in Lawton, as well as phoning RJ, but neither of them answered. His day had not started well at all.

But being able to take in the beautiful view of Becca heading toward him? Things were looking up.

She hadn't noticed him yet, so he took the opportunity to watch her. She bounced a little as she walked, obviously happy as she made her way back to the house. She'd wrapped her hair up in a messy bun, allowing little strands to brush over her cheeks from the slight breeze. Mike wanted to muss her up even more.

He took the porch deck steps down and when she caught sight of him, her grin grew. And that went straight to his heart. Shit, he wasn't supposed to getting so attached to her. His entire future was mixed up and unsettled. Having a little fun with her was one thing, but Mike was beginning to care about her. He wanted to that brilliant smile directed at him every morning. *What was he going to do?*

She met him in the middle of the yard and threw her arms around his neck. "What a great morning!"

He laughed. "Your house burned down the night before last."

She dropped back on her heels. "Oh, yeah. Well, today started out better than yesterday so that's something."

He gave her a quick peck on the mouth. "Keep that thought."

This time, she frowned and withdrew her arms. He didn't want to be the bearer of bad news, but they couldn't get lost in what was going on between them. There were some very dangerous people out there. Becca was an obvious target.

"What happened?" she asked.

"Owen's gone," he explained. "He's not on Pack lands, in town, or anywhere we've searched."

"Damn," she muttered. "Okay, well, he couldn't have gone far. We'll find him. This territory has a lot of land associated with it. Owen wouldn't have left the area without carrying out whatever mission he thinks he has."

"I agree," Mike said. "You need to be careful, though. He's already set his sights on you once."

"Of course. I'm not going to try to be a hero. I won't let anyone around me get hurt because I do something dumb."

"I left a message with a buddy of mine. He's great at tracking. If we don't locate him soon, I want him to come down and help." He slung his arm around her neck and started to lead her back to the house. "Now where did you disappear to this morning? I was hoping to get in some serious cuddling time."

Becca hip-checked him. "Yeah, I know what kind of cuddling you were thinking about. It's later than I thought. I was coming to wake you my own special way."

"Sorry I missed that then," he pouted.

She stopped and turned to face him. "I should tell you that I went and talked to Kurt."

Mike jerked back. Normally he would have had better control of himself but after their confessions the night before he hadn't thought Becca would leave his bed to see her ex. Fuck, he was stupid. Here he was stressing about how fast they were moving and the deep feelings he had and she was with another guy.

She grabbed his arms and pushed him to the side of the house. "Really? After everything that was said last night, you're going to doubt my intentions?"

He opened his mouth to deny her accusation, but she waved a hand. "What am I thinking? You're a man!"

Mike nodded. He was a man, but that was not what left him speechless. Oh, no. The sight of Becca fuming before him was hot. Shit, his cock had been half hard but now hurt from pressing into the zipper of his jeans. *What would she do if I haul her against the house and ravish her?*

She smacked his shoulder. "I told you last night I'd never told Kurt he was right. It was time he knew. Without him taking a stand, my dreams wouldn't have been possible, even if the cost was our relationship. He needed to hear from me that it was time he came back to the Pack to visit."

That couldn't have been an easy conversation to have. Damn, now he felt even more guilty for doubting her.

"As for your involvement, I don't want to start a relationship with you with that still hanging over our heads."

This was it. Becca was strong, brave and amazing. He was in trouble.

Her eyes sparkled as she braced her feet shoulder-width apart and fisted her hands on her hips. "Well? Don't you have anything to say?"

He licked his lips. "God, I could fall in love with you." Well shit, that wasn't what he'd meant to say. Mike tried to think of some way to cover his words. "I mean…that's to say…" He stopped talking. God, he was embarrassed.

Her expression softened. "I know. Me, too. That's why I had to talk to Kurt. I made mistakes in the past, letting what everyone else wanted become more important. You deserve better than that. If we don't work out, it won't be because my old boyfriend is standing over our heads."

Mike reached for her and she let him wrap his arms around her and pull her close. She'd been honest with him, so it was time to man up. Who cared if his hands were shaking and he had to clear his throat? He wanted her, plain and simple. Now he needed to make up for his asshole behavior. "I don't care that you went and talked to your ex. I was surprised. And maybe a little disappointed."

She raised an eyebrow. "Disappointed?"

"Yeah," he whispered as he ran his tongue down her neck. "I was looking forward to waking up with you in my arms. Cuddling, remember?"

She sagged in his hold and tilted her head back to give him better access. "Well…"

Turning them, Mike pressed her against the brick of the main house. He pressed close so she could feel his erection and rubbed himself over her. Her moan was long and deep. It appeared that she approved.

"Mmm." She shuddered. "That…that would have been nice."

"Nice?" he growled. "I think we can do better than nice."

He lifted her with hands on her hips so she was trapped between the wall and his body. She wrapped her legs around his waist while yanking at his shirt.

"Skin," she demanded. "I want your skin."

Mike helped her and pulled the shirt over his head, before dropping it to the grass. He rocked forward, drawing out another low long moan from her. "Here, baby? You want me to take you here where anyone can come up on us?" He wasn't opposed to the idea. After all, their first night in the woods had been extremely erotic. The cool night air, the chance of exposure, the smell of nature. He had a kinky side he hadn't even known about.

But this wasn't the same. This was her home.

"I want you," she exclaimed. "Yes, here, now."

No one could have said no to that. "Pull your shirt up," he ordered.

He positioned his hands to get a better hold on her. Becca lifted the hem of her shirt and unclasped her bra.

"Give me your breasts."

Cupping herself, she tilted forward. He licked her pert nipple before drawing the nub into his mouth. She arched, crying out.

God, he loved the sounds she made.

Nuzzling and sucking, he treated her other tit to the same treatment. Didn't stop until she was panting, begging for his cock. He would never make her beg, though. If Becca wanted, he would provide her with enough pleasure to make her weak in the knees.

"I need you," she declared.

He gently lowered her legs to the ground, making sure she was steady. Her shirt came off, her bra hung off one shoulder, and he was already working on her jeans. Mike shoved her pants past her knees and helped her fall forward onto the grass. She made a picture on her hands and knees. He stood above her and lowered his zipper.

"Fuck, baby, you are so hot. I'm gonna fill you. Take you so hard. You're going to be screaming my name," he promised.

She nodded. "Yes, please."

He shoved his own jeans and boxers down before dropping to cover her body with his. Mike used his fingers to make sure she was ready, slipping two digits inside. She rocked back against him. Even though he would have preferred more foreplay, they were already on dangerous ground being so close to the house.

"Ready?" He removed his hand and positioned the head of his cock at her entrance.

"Give it to me."

Mike meant to tease her. Resting the tip of his cock between her folds, he could already feel the wet heat of her pussy. Instead of him taking his time, Becca slammed herself back and took him in on one motion, her inner muscles squeezing his cock. He gripped her hip, groaning, trying to rein in his control. He loved being inside her and was already close to coming.

"Now, fuck me like you mean it," she ordered.

Mike drew back before slamming in again. "Demanding little thing," he huffed out, but his laugh was strained. No one else had ever challenged him this way. He rode her hard, thrusting into her.

Becca urged him on, calling out "Faster" and a string of *yeses*.

Her body tightened around him as her muscles clamped down while she climaxed. Becca shuddering and whimpering only heightened his own arousal. Mike pounded in harder. Thank God she could handle his frantic pace. The buzz under his skin alerted him to his own pending orgasm. He dropped his mouth to her shoulder and bit down as his seed pumped from his cock and released inside her.

They collapsed onto the damp grass, and she started to giggle. The happy sound made a chuckle escape him. He shifted off her and lay on his back, utterly exhausted. She propped up on an elbow.

"Now that was worth waiting for," she told him with a wink. "I think I might sneak out every morning if this is how you punish me."

He shook his head. The damn female was going to kill him. "I'll show you punishment," he threatened. Instead, he clasped her hand in his. He'd get up and get them inside soon. Well, when the small tremors still coursing through his body subsided.

* * * *

By the time she and Mike had been able to sneak back into the house, shower together, and dress for the second time, Becca's blood was humming. At least she would have the energy to deal with what was left of her cottage. Even though she had the apartment in town, she wanted her home fixed. It would mean spending some of the savings she'd put aside for her next trip, but the house was more important.

Becca strolled to the bed where Mike was glaring at his phone. Which hadn't rung, even though he'd checked it at least five times in the last ten minutes. She could feel the aggravation coming off him.

"They'll call," she told him.

He nodded but was still frowning. "I don't like being kept in the dark. We can't depend on the investigators, obviously. We don't know who Owen is working with. Every case could be tampered with. There are a lot of details and evidence that Owen had access to."

"You mean you think other members of the Pack could be involved?" she asked, although she didn't want to. Wasn't it bad enough that it looked like even one member of the Pack was involved? To have other members involved? God, that betrayal hit deep.

"It's possible. I'm sorry," Mike told her, cupping her cheek and placing a kiss on her forehead. "We have to look to see who he is involved with. We have to make sure. Brandon doesn't have jurisdiction here, but with pressure from the Alpha Council, I'm hoping he'll know what steps to take."

Becca pulled away and walked over to the window. She pushed the curtain back and gazed out onto her property, the territory she had grown up in. Surely the entire police force couldn't be involved? That would be devastating. "Why? Why would they do this? My father is a good and fair Alpha."

Mike wrapped his arm around her shoulders and squeezed tight. "I don't know. Some people are evil."

She sighed. *Can it be that simple? evil in the world? There has to be more to it than that, doesn't there?*

"Why our Pack?" she questioned. She knew that Mike didn't have the answers, but she needed to voice the question anyway.

"I don't know. But we will find out," he promised. "I believe it goes back to the humans. They might have something against the shifters helping them. Or perhaps convinced them. Either way, we'll get the answers you need."

She leaned back into his hold. That was all they could hope for. "Thank you. I want to talk to my dad before I call some contractors, regarding my cottage. I'm not going to leave it a pile of rubble."

He kissed the back of her head. "Let's go down and get to work."

She gladly twined her fingers with his. He lifted her hand and kissed her knuckles. The gesture was sweet and she felt like the luckiest girl in the world. Walking out of the bedroom, she glanced behind her to the unmade bed. Being back in the main house wasn't ideal, but they'd make do. At least no other guest room around them was being used. Becca led the way down the stairs, trying to make a mental list of what needed to be done. Her dad's office door was open and voices came from within. She didn't let go of his hand as they reached the threshold. Mike glanced over at her and she shrugged. It wasn't like they had to hide their relationship.

"Dad?" She knocked on the open door and went inside. Her father stood talking with Eric and Kenny, but he smiled at her when they entered the office. She released her hold on Mike, walking straight over to her dad. He opened his arms and she hugged him tight. Wrapping her arms around his waist, she buried her face in his chest. He'd always been so supportive of her. The previous night she'd acted like a spoiled brat. Kurt wasn't the only person she needed to apologize to. Peace settled over her as he rocked her. She was reminded how strong her father was. Tipping her head back she gazed up at him. "I'm sorry."

He shook his head. "No, you don't have to apologize," he said and glanced over at Mike. "I should have told you. I thought about it several times." He dropped his voice. "When I saw your attraction to Mike, I knew I couldn't. If you had known Kurt was back, would you have been able to get to know Mike?"

She peeked back at Mike, who was acting like he wasn't paying attention to them. She knew, though, that he could still hear every word, like Eric and Kenny could. But the other men in the room were doing their best to give her and her dad privacy.

"I think I would have," she admitted. "I really do."

He father beamed down at her. "I'm happy, right? I don't need to go all growly on him?"

She laughed. "Yes, you're happy, Dad."

He hugged her tight again. They let go of each other and her dad walked over to Mike. He held out his hand. When Mike accepted the handshake, her dad murmured, "I'm glad you came."

"Me, too," Mike agreed.

That taken care of, her dad turned back into the Alpha. "We have a lot to discuss."

Everyone took a seat—her dad behind the desk, Eric and Kenny in the two chairs in front of him, and Becca and Mike side by side on the couch.

"The fire at the cottage had the same accelerant as the others in town. It's the same people," Eric updated them. "I asked for copies of the police files. After talking to Mike at breakfast, we're concerned some of the evidence might be tampered with."

Her father sighed. "We're certain Owen is involved?"

"As much as we can be without talking to him. He's hiding somewhere. Hopefully no one in your Pack is helping him, but we can't be sure."

"The cabin the humans are in is still under surveillance. Owen's not there," Kenny informed them.

"The humans may not be involved," Eric noted. "Right now, all we know is they're not fond of shifters."

Mike shook his head. "With the timing of them showing up and what has been overheard, I can't see them not being involved."

Kenny nodded. "I agree with Mike."

Her dad leaned back in his chair. "I want Owen found. Let's keep an eye on the humans, but Owen is our priority. I don't know if he knew whether or not Becca was home but…" He shook his head.

Becca shivered thinking of the possibility that she could have been home alone.

"I saw him at the diner last night," Mike mentioned.

"I don't remember seeing him," Kenny said with a frown. "Damn, that makes me think he did believe Becca was home. And maybe you were with her."

"Seems you may be making someone nervous," Eric added.

"Yeah," Mike agreed.

"Send out as many of the men as you can to look for Owen. I want him located today. I need to call the council and give them an update. Becca, we have to go through the cottage today."

Everyone nodded.

Mike's cell phone rang and he looked at the screen. He nodded toward her dad. "I need to take this."

Her father waved him off. "Go ahead."

Mike walked out of the room and Becca couldn't help but let her gaze follow him. Once he'd walked out of the door, she looked back around and saw the three men watching her with amusement.

"Oh, shut up," she said with a laugh that broke the tension the previous conversation had brought to the room. "I want to start rebuilding right away."

"Are you sure?" her dad asked. "We can assign you another house."

"No." She shook her head. Becca had thought about it. "I'm going to use my savings. My cottage will be where it always was. It might not be the same. I'll upgrade now that I have the choice, but it's going back right there."

"You don't have to. Your mom—"

"Mom and you raised me there before you moved into the main house. I want it back."

"Okay." Finally, he gave in. "But I can help you pay for it."

She opened her mouth to argue, but he held up a hand. "I insist. There's some material I've been researching that is fire resistant. It wouldn't have saved everything, but I'd like to try it out. Your new home will give me the perfect opportunity."

Becca could argue with him for days, but he was stubborn. "Fine, but I want a hot tub."

Her father laughed. "I think we can handle that."

Mike answered Brandon's call as he stepped into the hallway. "Hello."

"Hey, man." Brandon Stratton's voice came through. "I got your message. I did a search through the council records on your guy. He doesn't have a criminal background, but I expected that, since he's a cop. But I did find something interesting."

"What?" Mike asked, excited at the chance of having a lead.

"He was raised by a human mother. He didn't join the Pack until he was in his mid-twenties. Five years ago, in fact."

"Well, that's different," Mike observed. It was rare for a child shifter to grow up outside a Pack. He had met shifters who had gone Rogue once they were adults, but it was unusual for a child to be without Pack. They needed the security and closeness other shifters offered while going through puberty.

"Yeah," Brandon agreed. "I did a search on the rest of the family. It appears that Owen's mom and dad were never married. I can't find much more on the dad other than a name on a birth certificate. It's like he disappeared."

Mike hummed. *Interesting.*

"The mom, however, did marry when Owen was five. Had two more children over the years," Brandon provided. "But here is where it gets interesting."

Mike leaned against the wall of the hallway. Becca and Kenny walked out of the office and she stopped next to him. He pulled her close to his side. "Go on."

"Owen's stepfather is Dan Carter," Brandon announced.

"Carter? The preacher that's been all over the television spouting hatred to all shifters?" How we're all abominations, evil, and creatures that are a threat to humans?" Mike asked, shocked. Becca stiffened beside him while Kenny frowned.

"Yes, that Carter," Brandon confirmed. "So, if Owen is involved, you can almost be guaranteed his followers are also."

"Damn, the humans that are in the cabin," Mike groaned. "This just got a whole lot more complicated."

"Watch your back," Brandon said. "He's a dangerous man. I'm sorry I got you involved in this."

"I'm not," Mike replied, his hold on Becca tightening.

"Really?" Brandon sounded amused. "Anything you'd like to share?"

"No."

"I'll have RJ get it out of you," Brandon teased. "He's better at storytelling than you, anyway."

Mike grunted in response. That was only true because his best friend was a drama king. "Speaking of RJ, I called him earlier and he still hasn't gotten back to me."

"I think Nikki came home late last night. You might not hear from him for a while."

"Gotcha," Mike laughed. "I'm going to update everyone here. Keep looking into the cops, if you can."

"Will do," Brandon promised.

"Thanks, man." He placed his phone in his back pocket after disconnecting.

"Dan Carter?" Kenny questioned.

Mike ran his hands over his face and looked up. Todd had come into the hallway from the kitchen and Alpha Nelson and Eric were now standing in the office doorway.

"We've got a huge problem," Mike explained what Brandon had learned.

Alpha Nelson started barking orders, placing the Pack on high alert. "I don't want anyone left alone until we figure this out."

Mike admired the way the man thought and dealt with issues.

"Yes, sir," Eric ran off.

"Kenny, update Kurt and the other men. Todd and Mike, I need you both to join the search for Owen — the need to get to him quickly is now even more urgent. Becca, start informing the Pack about the alert. I'm calling the council right now," Alpha Nelson said.

Mike kissed Becca before following Todd out to his SUV. He could tell that the younger shifter wasn't exactly thrilled with being partnered with him for the day, but Mike didn't care. There was no way he was going to let the crazy humans attack or hurt anyone else. He'd worked side-by-side with humans in the military for several years. He still remained friends with most of them. Even though they hadn't been part of his unit, they had saved his ass a few times.

When the Packs had become public, several humans he'd met over the years had reached out to him in support. For the most part, the majority of humans had been excited about the news. It was a shame that one small group of humans could cause so much distrust and tension between the shifters and the rest of the people.

Todd started the truck and glanced over at him.

Mike had planned to ignore Todd, but he'd had enough. "What exactly is your problem with me?" he asked.

Todd shook his head. "No problem," he murmured.

"Yeah, right," Mike scoffed.

Todd glared at him. "I've been friends with Becca all my life," he said.

So, the man was protective. Mike could appreciate that.

"Kenny has had to give up a lot for the Pack. He had to take his brother's place when Kurt decided not to stay," Todd went on.

"Okay," Mike responded, not sure now where Todd was going.

Todd turned to him. Mike saw the strong emotions in his eyes. "I don't to want to see my friend hurt. Becca's been left behind before. It's not fair to her." Todd dropped his head back on the seat and closed his eyes. "Man, I haven't seen her into anyone like this since…well, ever."

The confession made Mike feel good. Made his blood pump faster and the wolf inside him stretch with contentment.

"I want to see her happy," Todd finished.

"Hey, man," Mike said, "I'm not here to hurt her. Becca… Becca was unexpected. I never thought I'd see her again. Now that I have, I'm unprepared. I'll admit that. But I can guarantee I will not hurt her on purpose."

Todd nodded. "I guess that's all I can ask for."

Mike was glad Todd accepted his explanation. His relationship with Becca was moving fast, but he wasn't sure where that would lead.

"The thing is, Kenny found out about the two of you and started looking to the future. Excited for the first time in months," Todd stated.

Mike wasn't sure what that meant. "I don't understand…"

Todd sighed. "He'd kill me for telling you, but Kenny is hoping you stay around."

Mike shrugged. He hadn't thought about it, but if things progressed with Becca, it could be a possibility. Mike wasn't going to return to his home Pack. That he'd already decided.

"Kenny never wanted to be head of security for the Pack. He likes his position, but he doesn't feel that is his true place. He's a fireman to the core. Wants to become an arson investigator."

Mike remembered what Becca had told him and Todd's words started to make sense. "He wants me to take over for him?" he asked with a raise of his eyebrow.

Todd bit his lip in worry. The action showed how young the man was—at least ten years his junior. This had to be hard for him. "…maybe think about it."

Mike reached over and grasped his shoulder. "You're a good friend and a good…boyfriend?" No one had yet spoken the words out loud to him. But he'd been in the diner the previous evening. Todd and Kenny were in love.

Todd chuckled. "Yeah," he admitted, dropping his head. "Does that bother you?"

Mike patted his shoulder. "Nah, man. I think it's great. As long as you're good to each other and are committed to making things work. We should all be so lucky."

Todd blew out a breath. "Alpha Nelson knows. So do a few others. We haven't told the entire Pack, though. It shouldn't be a problem." He shrugged, "But you never know."

He didn't have the heart to tell him more people knew than they thought. Todd had a habit of marking Kenny with his scent. They weren't exactly covert. Still maybe he could say something to make Todd feel better. "I understand. But I have several friends who are involved in same-sex relationships. My unit leader is even mated to another man," he told Todd. He didn't mention that Casey's mate was also the feline Prince. "People are more accepting than you would think. And if they have a problem with it? Fuck them."

Todd grinned. "Yeah."

"Now let's find this asshole so we can get back to Kenny and Becca," Mike declared.

"You got it, man. I thought we would look close to the humans. If Owen is related to them, he might not be with them, but I would bet he is staying pretty close to the only support he has left."

"I like it," Mike approved.

Todd filled him in on several places that he wanted to check out as he drove. His plan would have them staying in town, since Kurt and his men had the outside pretty much covered.

It took twenty minutes to get to the first location.

"I would like to shift," Mike decided. They were far enough that he shouldn't be spotted by any humans. Kenny's warning about how much the tourists wanted to see a shifter stuck with him.

"Good idea," Todd agreed.

Mike opened his door and started to strip. He left his boots and socks on the floorboard and yanked off his shirt. He stood beside the SUV and shucked his jeans.

Todd stood at the back of the vehicle, keeping an eye out. Mike dropped to his knees, calling forward his wolf. His transformation gave him such a benefit compared to his human body. Even though his senses were heightened as a man, giving into the animal put him in the right frame of mind to hunt. He trotted over to Todd, nudging the man's hand.

"Ready?" Todd asked, giving him a scratch on the top of his head.

Mike let his tongue roll out then butted his head against Todd's side. Taking off, he challenged Todd to keep up.

Zigzagging through the dense trees, Mike concentrated on other shifter scents. A fair number of people had been through the area, but none of them recently. Mike could see why the town would use this path to take them farther into the forest.

If Owen came from the diner to here, it would have been late last night.

Too much time had passed for Mike to distinguish him from any others.

Moving still farther beneath the canopy, he kept his senses on alert. Owen could be anywhere close by. Mike didn't feel like he was being watched but didn't take chances. Not when Becca's safety was in danger.

Chapter Six

It had been a hard afternoon, but Becca knew the calls she'd made had been necessary. Sometimes having to be the one to remain calm and the one others looked at for answers was the hardest part of being the Alpha's daughter. Several years ago, she'd been held to a higher standard than other teens. She was the Alpha's daughter — the Pack's daughter — so what she did mattered. Everyone she spoke to asked about her cottage.

They'd also offered help. From construction supplies to labor, her Pack was showing their strength. They helped one another. Why Owen would betray them confused her.

Becca still remembered when Owen had come to the Pack. He'd petitioned to join and her father had given him a year's trial period. Owen had seemed to bloom from a lonely young guy to a man. The training with the police force had seemed to help Owen find a purpose.

She wouldn't say they were close friends, but she'd counted on Owen to protect her and the entire Pack. The betrayal stung. Becca couldn't even imagine how her father felt.

But thinking about Owen wasn't getting her any answers or helping her anxiety. She stood from the couch, stretching her arms over her head.

Becca glanced at her watch—almost dinner time. She hoped the teams that had headed out to search for Owen had had some luck. Becca was honestly scared now that they'd learnt Preacher Carter and his followers were involved. No knowing what Carter wanted terrified her. Her family had been targeted and the Pack needed to be careful. There'd been several humans who'd spoken out against shifters, but Carter's words had power to put them in real danger. He had enough followers to put up a fight. Carter wanted to gather all the shifters and corral them. Sometimes Carter claimed shifters needed to be destroyed while on other occasions he suggested putting them in prisons. No matter what Carter said, the future wouldn't be good for shifters if he got his way.

All the work the council and other shifter leaders had done before the announcement revealing their presence had been to avoid the reaction Carter was stoking.

The man made her sick.

She left the living room that she had taken over to get her calls made and walked to her dad's office. The door was closed, so she knocked until she heard his command to enter. He glanced up at her when she walked in and, although he looked tired, he smiled at her.

"How's it going, Dad?" She moved around the desk to hug him.

He sighed. "Better now."

She grinned at him before taking a seat in the chair in front of him. "Did you talk to the council?"

"Yes, and they are very worried about what Carter and his congregation's connection means. And why we were targeted when there are bigger and more public Packs out there."

"Do they have a theory?" she asked.

If anyone could figure it out, it had to be the council, eight powerful, dominant wolves who at one time had been Alphas of their own territories. The experience and knowledge that the council brought to the Packs was undeniable. The wolves were lucky to have them. The several shifter species had different ways to support and govern themselves. It was one of the reasons they had received such support from the world's leaders. They had existed in secret for so long because they followed the laws of their species.

The felines followed a royal line, the bears and most water species had a dominance order, and the birds were fashioned after the military. Most, however, had a small group of leaders. Like the wolves' Alpha council.

"Their fear is that as we're the Pack closest to the council, they may be the ultimate target," her dad informed her.

She couldn't contain her gasp. "They wouldn't really go after the council, would they? Beside it's not common knowledge where they're located."

Her dad's shoulders drooped. "It's not impossible to discover the whereabouts of the council compound. Carter had a lot of resources at his disposal. I believe they would target our leaders to hurt all shifters. The council has already gotten involved by asking for help for us. That's why Mike is here."

"So, if something were to happen to Mike?" She wasn't able to finish the thought. "Oh, God!"

He nodded. "I know. I sent Kenny to find Mike and Todd and get them back here. We need to come up with a better plan than randomly searching through the woods. Plus, they need back up."

Becca's pulse picked up and her wolf scratched to get out and protect Mike. She fisted her hands and took deep breaths, trying to calm herself.

A hand gripped hers and she opened her eyes to see her dad kneeling in front of her.

"Calm down, sweetie. It will be okay," he soothed her.

It took several minutes, but she got herself under control.

"Good girl," he praised. "You really like this guy?"

"I do. I met him when Nikki mated with RJ. There was something about him that called to me."

He smiled. "I think his dominance might have something to do with that. He's trustworthy, as well. And he came to help out a Pack that he didn't even know."

"So, you like him?"

"Are you asking my approval?" He raised an eyebrow.

Am I? "No, not really. I guess I'm wondering if you think this is a bad idea? That I'm getting ahead of myself."

"Who cares if you are?" he asked. "You're allowed to follow your heart, even if it means being disappointed in the end. We all go through this uncertainness."

"Did you with Mom?"

"I wasn't sure I wanted to settle down. But your mother was a force of nature. She rolled into town and swept me up. I didn't stand a chance."

Becca smiled. She was lucky that her dad didn't mind talking about her mom. The pain he felt by her death would never go away, but Becca needed to talk about her sometimes. "I didn't think I'd ever see him again. Or maybe if we were both visiting Nikki and RJ at the same time, we might have. I didn't expect him to come here."

"I spoke to Nikki's brother before he asked Mike to help. Brandon was under the impression that Mike needed something to keep him busy."

"Yeah, I can't see him doing well being bored."

"Sounds like someone else I know." Her father stared down at her.

So Mike and I do have a lot in common. That has to count for something.

The phone on the desk rang, and her dad rose to answer it. "Hello?"

Kenny's panicked voice came over the line. Becca jumped up, overhearing her friend's fear. "Alpha! I found Todd's vehicle, but there's no sign of him or Mike. I've got Ryan and Adam out here, but the scent is at least a couple hours old. There...there are signs of struggle."

Her dad's eyes met hers. "Where?" he demanded.

Kenny gave him directions while her dad scribbled down the information.

"Find Kurt and have him help you search. I'll send more of the Pack. We'll find them." He was hanging up as she raced to the door.

"No."

She whirled around. "What?"

"You're not going," he said. He already had the phone back in his hand.

"I am," she argued.

He didn't respond, instead barking out orders for more guards around the house and everyone else available to get to Todd and Mike's last location.

Becca began to pace as she waited. She didn't like being put on the back burner, but her father did have to organize a rescue. When finally her dad gave her his attention, his lips were set in a firm line.

"I need you to stay here," he said.

"Why?" Becca threw her hands up. "I could help."

"Because this could be a ploy to get to you."

"I don't care," she declared.

"Well, I do."

"You can't actually stop me," she claimed. Becca was itching to run out. She needed to do something to help.

"I can. I'll have the guards lock you in if I have to."

"You wouldn't!" Becca knew her father was protective, but this was too much.

He grunted. That wasn't a good sign.

"Please, Dad."

"I'll make you a deal." He waited for her nod. "Let the others go out first. Give them a couple of hours. If they haven't found them, you can join the search."

Becca glanced at her watch. "Two hours. After that, I go."

"Fine," he agreed.

Okay, so she had to hope the others came through. She could do that. And if Todd and Mike weren't found, she'd tear the town apart looking for them.

* * * *

Becca paced in front of the window in her dad's office. For over two hours, Kenny had led the group looking for Todd and Mike. Mike's scent covered a wide area, so Becca figured he had been in his wolf form at some point. Todd's scent was only located close to his SUV.

Now the teams were about to spread out to expand their search. Becca was done with waiting. "I'll meet up with Kenny."

"I don't like you going out there," her father replied. "There's too much ground to cover. You'll be vulnerable."

"Whoever took Mike and Todd have already had them for two hours! I'm not waiting any longer." She stomped to the door. Yanking it open, she almost plowed into the guard who'd been about to knock.

"Ugh." He stumbled. "I have a couple of shifters at the door asking for Mike or you, Becca," the guard said.

She glanced over her shoulder at her father. Why would anyone be asking for her?

"What're their names?" her dad demanded.

"RJ Cross and Nikki Stratton," the guard replied.

Becca cried out and raced from the room. Her dad called her name, but she was almost to the door by the time footsteps sounded behind her. She yanked the door open and launched herself at her friend.

Nikki caught her and laughed. As they hugged, the anxiety of the last few hours caught up with Becca. She sobbed onto her friend's shoulder, reliving the entire ordeal starting with the first fire. Finally, there was someone around she didn't have to be strong with.

"What's wrong?" Nikki asked.

Becca shook her head, unable to speak. She needed a minute to get control of herself. She took a deep breath.

"Hey." Nikki drew her back. "What is it?"

"Mike's missing," she blurted out. "As well as one of my best friends."

"What?" RJ demanded.

Nikki shushed him as a commotion at the door caught their attention. Becca's dad and a couple of guards joined them. Becca waved in the direction of her father. "My dad, the Alpha."

"Jim Nelson," her dad introduced himself.

RJ grasped his hand. "Sir, RJ Cross. And I believe you've met my mate, Nikki Stratton."

Nikki accepted a hug from Jim.

"Let's bring this inside," her dad ordered and led the way back to his office.

They filed down the hall until they'd returned to the Alpha's office. "I wasn't aware we were expecting company," her dad commented.

"My fault, sir," Nikki said. "I was in a rush to get here and didn't have a chance to call."

"I'm sorry, Alpha, but what is this about Mike missing?"

"I guess we could use some help," her dad stated. "Let's get you two caught up."

Becca sat on the couch next to Nikki and RJ. She explained to them what they had found out so far. Once she was done, RJ slumped back and ran his hands over his face.

"Damn." RJ rose and paced to the window.

"We're not sure when they were taken. It looked like they got Todd by the vehicle, but Mike's scent sort of disappears," Alpha Nelson explained.

RJ nodded. "That doesn't mean he was taken, though. We got good at hiding our scent in the military."

Becca perked up. "You mean he may be out there and okay?"

RJ grinned at her. "I would bet on it. Mike's good. One of the best in his animal form. If he was shifted when they attacked, there is no way they got the upper hand."

"But Todd?" Becca asked. "He wouldn't have let them get him."

RJ held up a hand. "If he saw Todd get taken and wasn't able to do anything about it, he'd have followed them. Until he could return for help."

"We need to find him," Becca said. "He may need us."

RJ scanned the room. "I know how Mike works." He turned his attention to her dad. "With your permission, sir."

The Alpha nodded. "Just watch over my daughter."

"Yes, sir," RJ responded. "You know how to get where we're going?"

Becca nodded at his question. "Let's go." She grabbed the keys to one of the Pack's explorers.

RJ wasn't messing around. Before they were even out the door, he was phoning someone named Casey. Becca was too distracted to even listen in.

"What're you doing here, anyway?" she asked Nikki when they reached the SUV.

RJ climbed in the back while Nikki took the passenger side.

"Mike called RJ about needing a tracker. I already wanted to come so we decided to head down."

Of course, Mike had been talking about one of his former unit members when he'd told her about calling in help. She hadn't expected it to be RJ. "Well, I'm glad you came." She started the vehicle.

Nikki patted her arm. "How're you holding up?"

Becca laughed. "I'm thinking I need a long vacation on a beach somewhere with one of those drinks that has a little umbrella."

"Yeah." Nikki was already nodding. "Maybe some greased-up cabana boys to service you."

"Yes!" Becca hissed. "What a good idea."

"You know I can hear you," RJ groused from the back seat. He'd hung up from his call and was scowling at them. "And Becca has Mike's scent all over her."

Becca froze. No one said anything until Nikki leaned over and sniffed her.

"Stop that." Becca pushed her friend away. "That's creepy."

"You do smell like Mike," Nikki commented. Then she glared toward the back seat. "You and your super nose. That's weird."

RJ shrugged. Becca could see him smiling though from the rearview mirror.

"Training," RJ quipped.

That comment reminded her about what RJ had said about Mike. Maybe she was panicking for no reason. RJ was Mike's best friend, so if he thought Mike would be okay, she had to have as much faith in her lover.

"So, Becca," Nikki drawled. "Anything you want to talk about?"

"Nope," Becca replied. "Not a thing."

Nikki was peering at her from the corner of her eye. "Oh, my God! This isn't the first time, is it? You totally hooked up with Mike when you were in town!"

"What?" she squeaked. "That's crazy." Damn, how had Nikki figured that out?

RJ barked out a laugh. "I told you!"

Nikki didn't respond to her mate, though. She was now staring at Becca. "You did!"

Becca sighed. There was no fighting admitting the truth, especially now that she and Mike had been so open about their relationship since he'd arrived. "Okay, yes. I didn't think I'd ever see him again. It was a surprise, but there is something between us."

RJ clapped his hands together. "This makes me so happy!"

Becca was almost used to RJ's childlike enthusiasm, almost. "Why's that?"

"You have no idea how long Mike has been giving me shit about Nikki. I finally get to give it back," RJ stated.

"I don't think Mike's quite as...in love as you are," Nikki teased.

"Whipped, you mean?" Becca taunted.

RJ growled. "Just for that, I'm not going to share any of Mike's embarrassing stories."

"Oh, come on!" Becca protested. "I was kidding."

RJ crossed his arms over his chest.

Becca looked over at Nikki. "Help me wear him down."

Nikki nodded.

"But we're here now, so it'll have to wait," Becca said. She pulled up and parked next to another vehicle. Kurt was already waiting when they pulled up next to Todd's SUV.

Becca jumped out and ran over to him. "Any word?" she asked.

Kurt shook his head. "No, I'm sorry."

Becca's shoulders slumped. Damn it, they needed to find Todd and Mike quickly. Nikki came up beside her and threw her arm around Becca's neck. "We'll find them."

"We damn sure will," Kenny muttered, joining them with RJ.

"RJ Cross." RJ held his hand out to Kurt.

"Kurt Moore. I've heard good things about you," Kurt greeted.

RJ raised an eyebrow.

"We have mutual friends and mutual training," Kurt shared. "Casey."

"Ah, well, then we're happy to have you along. I want to take a quick look before we all go out," RJ said.

Kurt jerked his head to the side and the two men walked off. RJ was only a few feet away when he started to pull his shirt over his head. Becca looked away. It didn't seem right to see Mike's friend in the buff. Even under the circumstances. RJ was an attractive man although she preferred the sleekness of Mike's body.

"Let's look around," Nikki suggested and started toward Todd's ride.

Becca peeked into the window. Mike's clothes were still locked inside. He had been in shifted form. Hopefully whoever attacked hadn't captured him. If Carter was involved, there was no telling what he'd do to a wolf. The preacher didn't see them as human at all. A shifter might be killed without questions asked. Her stomach rolled in despair.

Kenny was pacing in front of the spot where Todd had been taken. Every couple of minutes he breathed in deeply. She strolled over to him.

"This doesn't make sense," Kenny murmured. "If Todd was looking out for Mike, why would he let anyone get this close to him?"

Becca had the same question. "It had to be someone he knew," she guessed. "Maybe he thought they were here to help?"

Kenny shook his head. "He knew the possibility of someone from the Pack being involved."

Becca placed her hand in his. "Todd's strong. He'll make it through this. They haven't killed anyone yet."

"Yes," Kenny spat. "Shit, this is all my fault."

"No, it's not."

"He's put up with so much. Waiting on me when I had to take my position with the Pack. Having to hide our relationship. I love him."

Becca had known how Kenny felt but was glad he had finally said it out loud. "He knows that," she assured him.

"I hope so," Kenny whispered. He straightened his shoulders when RJ, in wolf form, came back with Kurt.

"This way." Kurt waved them over. The three of them hurried to him. "Clint's already in wolf form ahead of us. We'll shift and let RJ see if he can figure out where Mike would have gone. I think his theory that he followed the others makes sense. And shifted, he wouldn't have the ability to get help unless he backtracks here."

"Let's go then," Kenny demanded and started forward.

Kurt grabbed his shoulder. "I know this is hard for you, but we will find him."

Kenny jerked away and squinted at him. "What do you mean?"

Kurt shrugged. "Do you think I don't know about your and Todd's relationship?"

Kenny paled and stepped back farther.

Kurt's face fell. "Don't—"

"I don't... What... I mean..."

Kurt moved quickly, wrapping his hands around Kenny's upper arms. "It's okay. I suspected you had feeling for him before I left. I like Todd. I'm glad you found someone to love."

Kenny's mouth opened and closed as if he didn't know what to say.

Kurt glanced over at Becca with raw emotion in his eyes. She swallowed hard, realizing it looked like regret.

"We should all have what you and Todd do. You're a very lucky man. Don't throw that away. I'll support you both if you need me. And if anyone gives you trouble, I'll rip their fucking head off."

Kenny laughed before grabbing his brother and hugging him tight. "Thanks."

Kurt patted his back. "So, let's go get him."

They moved quietly to the covered area, so they could shift. Kurt dropped behind to walk with Becca. She allowed everyone else to move out of hearing range.

"I'll find him for you," he whispered.

Becca frowned. "What's going on, Kurt?"

Kurt shook his head. "Nothing. I want you to know I will get Mike back to you. And return Todd to my brother. I can see how much they mean to both of you."

"It's complicated—"

"You don't have to tell me. In fact, it's probably better you don't. I'm the ex, after all."

"I thought we agreed to be friends," she said.

"Yeah," Kurt agreed. "I hope we'll be able to do that."

"Then talk to me," she pleaded.

Kurt stopped walking, so she did, too. "It's weird being back here, that's all. At one time, I thought that I'd spend the rest of my life protecting this Pack."

"Is that what you want?"

"Look what's been happening while I've been gone," Kurt said. "Maybe if I'd–"

"No," she corrected him. "I'll not let you blame yourself for this."

Kurt looked around. "I let a lot of people down when I stayed in the military. My own brother thinks I'll turn on him because of who he loves."

"It's not you," she assured him. "Kenny has always been very private. He doesn't want to lose the respect of anyone in the Pack."

"That's not a concern he should have. He's made sacrifices for his people."

"I know. He'll have more support than he thinks when he and Todd finally step out. Plus, they're not as discreet as they believe. Everyone who is around them already knows."

Kurt chuckled. "He's grown up so much. I missed a lot."

That was in part her fault. "You don't have to any longer. Why not come back?"

"I can't."

"You can," she argued.

"I have other responsibilities now."

"What's that mean?" she asked. Kurt pressed his lips together then peered over her head in the direction the others had disappeared in. Becca grabbed the front of his shirt. "What are you talking about? You got a mate and pup hiding somewhere?" Surely Kurt would have at least told his family if that was the case.

Kurt chuckled. "No, nothing like that."

"Then?" she pressed.

"Things aren't going as well as the council hoped. Humans are rallying together against us. I've been recruited to work closely with the council."

"Oh." Becca was disappointed. She'd been hoping that Kurt would find his way back to his family.

"I'll make it a point to visit more often, though."

Becca gazed at him. This wasn't the same man she'd spent so much of her time with. He'd changed and Becca didn't know what he was thinking any longer. She didn't know this man. Still, something bothered her. "There's more, isn't there?"

He shook his head. "I've seen a lot of things in this world. When I joined the military, it was supposed to be to receive training to better help the Pack."

"You excelled, though."

"I did. Now, I don't think that I can give it up. It's not only what the council needs from me. I'm having trouble relating to other civilians. I'm struggling to find my place. The council's offer is what's best for now."

"Then do it," she said. "I'll support you and I know my dad and Kenny will, as well." Becca wondered if that was what Mike felt. Would he need something more than a Pack to protect?

"You're still so easy to read," Kurt commented. "I don't think Mike is in the same boat. He's restless, but he only needs to serve a purpose. He has a strong bond to the men he served with. Having something to do, someone to care for, and access to his friends will keep him happy."

"Don't you have that, as well?"

"No." Kurt frowned. "Most of my missions were solo or with one other guy. I have Clint and he's who I trust."

How sad. A wolf shifter needed the bond they formed through the Pack. Kurt had lost that.

"Don't be feeling sorry for me," Kurt said. "I'll figure it out. It's nice to see that while I might be a little lost, things here were going okay. I'm going to take out this threat to the Pack and you. Then I'll move on."

"I guess we should get going," she said.

"Yeah." Kurt hugged her. "Your man is out there waiting."

Becca jogged behind until they reached where everyone else had stopped. RJ stood closest to them as they approached. He was frowning at her before glaring at Kurt. She didn't know what that had been about, so she ignored it for now. They might have held the group up for a few minutes, but she didn't care. There was a lot going on and Mike would understand. She avoided eye contact with RJ as they all moved to a secluded spot to begin to strip.

Once in wolf form, Becca stretched her legs, happy with the release. She wiggled and pawed the ground.

Kurt's big tan wolf came up to her and laid his head against hers. She looked into his blue eyes and saw sadness. Then he was bounding away, racing deep into the trees.

They followed as a group, keeping their senses open to the area around them.

After ten minutes, by Becca's guess, they came upon a beautiful large white wolf. Pure white, his fur glistened in the sunlight, and Becca was impressed.

Kurt shifted back to human form at the same time as Clint did.

"Clint, any sign of them?"

Clint shook his head. "I lost his scent here. It's so strange, since there is nothing around. No way he could have been taken without the human leaving a trail. I can't figure it out."

RJ sniffed the ground and huffed. In a few moments, he was in human form also.

"He's hiding his scent. But if you know what you're looking for, he's also leaving clues. We've been through this before," he informed him.

Becca, Nikki and Kenny were in animal form still, so she was glad when Clint asked what the rest must be wondering.

"How is that possible? I've never heard of anyone hiding their scent before. I thought we had the same training?"

RJ grinned and waved to the tree. "We learned it from the felines. It's actually easy to master." RJ shifted again and went over to a tree. He scratched and rubbed himself against the wood then buried his head into the grass around the base.

It seemed to take forever with RJ covering every piece of ground around him, rolling around like a kid playing.

He trotted back to the group and lay in the middle of them.

Becca drew a deep breath and *yes*! While she could still smell some of RJ, if she hadn't been concentrating, she'd mostly have scented nature around them.

That was why Mike's trail seemed so old. He was burying himself beneath what was already around.

Getting excited, she scratched at the dirt, trying to tell the others she understood.

Clint and Kurt looked at RJ in amazement. Becca wanted to laugh. RJ was showing off a bit. He also appeared to be having a good time. Still they were much closer to finding Mike, so she didn't care.

"Damn." Clint cleared his throat. "That's awesome."

RJ climbed back up to his four feet and shook. He was ready to move on. Becca agreed.

"We'll follow you," Kurt told RJ. Kurt and Clint shifted back one more time. If that had been Becca, she would have been too exhausted to transform that many times. Every change affected both the human and animal half of their bodies.

RJ raced ahead, so Becca stayed right on his heels, with Nikki and the others close behind. It wasn't until they'd woven their way through miles of forest that RJ began to slow. Becca tried to be cautious as she crept forward. She didn't have the training the men did, but she knew how to walk silently in her environment.

As wolves, they followed behind RJ. Becca could barely contain her own animal need to race forward and find the men.

They moved slowly, RJ crossing over his own scent several times, before heading north and picking up speed.

Clint stayed by Nikki and Kenny, while Becca and Kurt matched RJ's pace.

Becca was starting to tire when RJ stopped and ducked his head. She and Kurt fell back and let him take a further lead. They wove around trees and fallen branches until an old metal shed came into view. RJ crouched and the other five took cover a few feet away. Becca lay on the ground and panted, trying to listen for any sounds of Mike or Todd.

The sound of a twig breaking had her head shooting up and she turned and looked across from her. The shadow moved and the big form headed to her. She wiggled, unsure what to do. If she made any noise to warn the others, the other wolf would hear her as well.

Her legs braced — she was ready to launch herself up.

The wolf stopped, gazing at her. Becca did let out a whimper this time.

She would have known those eyes anywhere.

Chapter Seven

Mike had heard the fast-moving Pack getting close to his location and had braced himself for attack. He used every ounce of stealth he had to cross over his trail to come up behind them. When they stopped, he crouched then moved closer.

He needed to get help, but he didn't want to leave Todd. He'd heard Todd's shout, the warning, before the sound of struggle had reached him. Todd had warned him off, but Mike couldn't leave the man to fend for himself. Now, he wasn't sure if he had been spotted or not.

The sun was starting to set and he knew Becca would be going crazy now that so much time had passed and he and Todd had not checked in. His first instinct when following the men who had taken Todd had been to cover his scent. It was something he had been taught back in the military.

He hoped that wouldn't keep anyone from looking for them.

Mike wished he could contact Kenny, or Kurt and his men, and especially Becca, but he knew he couldn't take the chance of them moving Todd, and him not knowing where they went.

As he'd followed the van, he'd expected them to head to the cabin that was under surveillance. They hadn't — instead, they had gone south and ended up at an old metal building that was almost falling down. They'd carried Todd out of the van and inside. Mike wanted to get a closer look but needed the cover of night to be sure he wasn't seen.

Now, there were wolves close to his location.

He knew they wouldn't be there for him and Todd. Not yet, anyway. Even as good as Kurt and his men probably were, they wouldn't be able to follow the clues. Only someone who'd been trained could do that.

He was hoping Becca would be worried enough to contact Nikki and RJ. RJ would know what he was doing. Mike figured they would be there early the next afternoon. He had to make sure Todd stayed okay for that long.

He crawled on his belly until he could see the first of the Pack.

A twig crunched under his paw and he froze.

A head popped up and he met the frightened gaze of another shifter. She wiggled and looked ready to pounce. He lowered his head, staring her down. *Becca*, he wanted to howl in relief. How in the hell had she gotten all the way out here, though? Was she a prisoner of the other wolves? He was not going to let them harm her.

She whined, which drew the attention of the Pack. Mike prepared himself to attack.

One of the big males noticed him and placed his body over hers. Mike couldn't tell who it was, but he didn't like it at all. She squirmed under the weight and whined while the male bared his teeth at him.

Mike growled deep in his throat.

"Stop!" The sharp order was quiet but still commanding.

Mike froze and glanced at the speaker. His mouth dropped. A naked RJ Cross stood between him and the other wolves.

Damn, guess I'm rescued after all.

He called forward his human side and, once he was no longer a wolf again, he stood to his full height. The male had moved off Becca, who had started to change back herself. The others followed suit. Once Becca was standing in front of him, he opened his arms and she rushed to him. He wrapped his arms around her while she buried her face in his chest.

She pulled away and peered up at him. "Are you okay?"

He nodded and kissed her forehead. "I'm fine." His voice was still rough from his previous form. He looked over at the others. RJ and Nikki stood with smiles on their faces watching them. Kenny and Clint were there, and Kurt, the male who had covered Nikki in protection, looked embarrassed.

With his arm still wrapped around Becca's shoulder, he walked over to the group.

RJ clasped hands with him while pulling him away from Becca and into a hug. "Good to see you, man."

Mike grinned. "That was quick. I didn't expect anyone to contact you so soon after I went missing. I figured you'd be here in the afternoon tomorrow."

RJ chuckled. "We were already here. Nikki got home about the time you left your message. There was a flight right away, so we had to scramble to get on it. I didn't have a chance to call. Arrived in town to find out that you'd done a disappearing act."

Mike punched RJ's shoulder. "Good timing. It's good to see you all. Truly."

He shook RJ's hand again, kissed Nikki's cheek and moved to shake with Clint and Kurt. Kurt looked surprised but relieved. Then he walked over to Kenny and lowered his voice even more. "Todd's not hurt. I think they knocked him out or something, but I didn't see or smell any blood. Haven't heard anything since they went inside, so I think he's still probably out."

Kenny relaxed a bit. "Thanks, man."

Mike waved everyone over into a circle. First, they needed to figure out a plan then he could relax and rest. He was fucking tired. "Okay, I'm pretty sure that the other cabin of humans was a distraction. From what I've seen, there are eight men here — all humans — along with two wolves who are helping."

"Two?" Kenny questioned.

Mike nodded. "Sorry, man, but it's the young guard from the house. I forget his name. Black hair, black goatee, with the big nose?"

"Barry?" Becca gasped. "No way Barry is involved."

"He is," Mike guaranteed her. "He drove up to Todd and rolled his window down. Todd was suspicious and kept his distance. He got hit with a dart from the back seat. Owen."

Kenny cursed and balled his hands into fists. "I'll take them apart."

Kurt patted his brother's shoulder. "I'll help."

Mike nodded with approval. The brothers had bonded in his absence. "And right after they took Todd in, Dan Carter left and hasn't been back." That was important information to have. When they got Todd back they would know for sure who was leading the assault on the Pack.

"So he is involved," Kurt confirmed. "These have to be his followers then."

"Yeah, I think they are using the group we found as a cover. Owen would know we were watching them. No one knew about this group. Or why they are here."

"The council," Becca said. "They're the target. My father believes that's why Owen went after Todd and Mike. The council sent Mike here. Maybe they thought Mike would lead them to their compound."

Mike dropped his head into his hands. "What a fucking mess," he mumbled.

"So, what's the plan?" Kenny looked back at the building that held his man.

Kurt grinned and rubbed his hands together. "Wait the couple hours till dark and hit them hard," he suggested.

RJ laughed. "Love it."

Nikki rolled her eyes, but she was also smiling. "They just want to fight."

RJ stuck his bottom lip out in the worst pout ever. "It's been so long, baby. You never let me have fun anymore. Pllllease!"

Nikki waved him off. "Fine. If you all can't take eight humans and two wolves, I don't know that I want you as my mate, anyway."

RJ wrinkled his nose at her. "What are you going to be doing?"

Mike loved the easy banter between the two. He peeked down at Becca, who still held his hand. She didn't seem to want to let go. He approved.

Nikki scoffed. "Isn't it obvious? While you guys are acting all macho and distracting everyone, me and Becca are going to rescue Todd."

Clint chuckled. "I think I like you all."

Everyone laughed at that.

"I guess now all we can do is wait," Kenny said and looked over his shoulder at the building in worry.

"Then we'll kick their asses," Kurt promised his brother. "I'll let you have the first punch."

Kenny sighed and Kurt patted his arm. Kenny moved over so he could watch the building while sitting back against a tree. Kurt and Clint settled several yards away keeping an eye out, too.

RJ tilted his head behind them and Mike nodded. He squeezed Becca and followed his friend farther into the brush. Becca and Nikki walked over to a fallen log where they huddled together. It was hard to tear his gaze from Becca.

"Come on," RJ urged.

Mike turned to follow his friend. Once they were far enough away from the others, RJ stopped. From this distance, if they whispered, they wouldn't be overheard.

"So…you and Becca, huh?"

Mike nodded. "It was unexpected," he admitted. "It's good, though."

"Is it serious?" RJ asked and crossed his arms over his chest. "You'll consider moving here, becoming part of her Pack, and stop traveling?"

Mike was confused. He'd thought RJ would be happy for him. "Maybe. Why?"

RJ sighed. "Sorry, man. I'm happy for you, it's…"

"What?" Mike snapped, pissed his friend would have a problem with Becca when he had always supported him and Nikki. Sure, Mike gave RJ a difficult time about how fast and hard his friend had fallen for Nikki, but it was done with love.

"Kurt's in love with her," RJ told him. "I don't think anything is going on between them, but it's obvious he has feelings for her. I don't want to see you hurt. We don't know much about her, if you think about it."

Mike blew out a breath. "I know all about Kurt's feelings for her."

RJ lifted an eyebrow. "You do? And he's still standing?"

Mike nodded and glanced at the man in question. Kurt was speaking with Clint and not paying attention to them. Even though there had been jealousy before, Mike felt more settled than he'd been since the day they all exited the military. He only hoped that this wasn't a passing attraction that Becca would soon regret. He was putting a lot of faith into a relationship that had only begun a few days ago. "I trust her."

"Enough to take a chance she might still have feelings for him?"

"They dated a few years ago, were even going to mate," he explained. "Kurt broke it off and rejoined the military, giving Becca the freedom she needed. He sacrificed his own happiness to give her a chance at a real future. One she actually wanted."

RJ gasped. "Shit. He's a good guy. That complicates things."

Mike shrugged. "Not really. It didn't work out between them. He left and she hasn't seen him since. It's my arms that she runs to."

"You're certain?"

"She doesn't love him anymore. I don't know if she would have even gone through with the mating. But I know how she feels about me. I'm not worried."

RJ slapped his back. "Well, then, damn, man, I'm thrilled for you. Becca is a great girl."

Mike knew he was grinning from ear to ear. That was the reaction that he'd expected. "I know."

"I can't wait to tell everyone!" RJ told him. He was bouncing on his toes. "Casey owes me a hundred bucks."

"What was the bet?" Mike wasn't even upset that his friends had been betting on him. He was used to their antics.

"I said that you'd find a girl and would be joining her Pack within a year. That was two months ago."

"What was Casey's take?"

"You'd be too stubborn to admit the attraction and it would take at least two years."

"You realize that I haven't joined a Pack, right?" Mike asked.

"It's a matter of time," RJ told him. "I know how you operate. You wouldn't be allowing everyone to know your business if you didn't care for her."

Mike grunted.

RJ motioned over to where Nikki and Becca were sitting close together with their heads bent so they could talk. "How much you want to bet they're talking about you?"

Mike punched RJ's arm. "Not taking that bet. I'm not a sucker. And you have a gambling problem."

"Only if I lost," RJ stated. "I don't lose."

He could only roll his eyes. "I'm going to talk to Becca and relax. It's been a long fucking day."

They walked back over to the girls. Mike sat behind Becca then pulled her close. She was shivering.

"Are you cold?" he asked rubbing his hands up and down her arms. "Maybe you should shift back."

He didn't mind his nakedness, but Becca might not be as comfortable. They should have brought clothes with them. Had no one been thinking?

She peered over her shoulder at him. "Not cold," she said with a wink. "Not now, anyway."

Mike chuckled. "Well, we don't have time for that," he told her, catching her meaning. "I guess I'll just have to sit here with you."

She leaned back against him. "It's okay. As long as you hold me."

Mike settled in for the wait. While the others kept watch, he could unwind. RJ would never allow Nikki to be put in danger, so Mike felt safe. Slowly the sun disappeared, dropping the temperature with it.

"Why don't you shift?" he said. "Then you can crawl in my lap and keep me warm."

"Okay," Becca agreed. She started the transformation. Nikki rose as well, following suit. Mike glanced at RJ. His friend never took his eyes from his mate. Was that what being in love would do to him? As much as Mike teased RJ, he was jealous that his best buddy had found such happiness. While Mike floundered with what to do next, RJ had his family, his mate and his tattoo shop. Maybe he should give his own family more time. Mike only went home when summoned by his parents. He didn't connect with them. After being in the worst possible situations, formal dinners and polite conversation bored him.

He couldn't put on a tux or thousand-dollar suit when he preferred fatigues or faded jeans. Back home,

Mike was always judged for how he dressed and spoke. No one wanted to spend time with him. Not even his parents. If he wasn't there to reflect well on him, they preferred he didn't show up.

Becca whined before pawing his leg, no doubt picking up on his distressing thoughts. Mike pulled her into his lap then began to stroke her soft fur. Mike chuckled. He'd never quite spent his downtime during a mission like this.

As the night came alive around them, the excitement started to fill the air. Becca tried to remain calm. She wasn't used to being in the middle of whatever the hell this was. She took photos for a living. Becca hid behind the lens, watching the world move one click at a time.

Mike stayed relaxed, holding her to his body.

He seemed to be lost in thought at times while stroking her hair. Becca wished she could see into his head. Mike didn't come across as being big on talking. In her experience, most men weren't especially if they were as dominant as Mike. Still, there was something that made her want to push him until he shared what was on his mind.

However, this wasn't the time. Not when they could be attacked at any moment. Or when Todd's life was at risk.

The moon still hung low when they heard a shout from inside the building.

Kenny jumped up and the only reason he didn't charge inside was because Kurt was able to grab him and hold him back. Mike leapt to his feet, blocking Becca from seeing the building. While she appreciated not be in the direct line of risk, Becca still wanted to see what was happening. She peered around Mike's hip.

"Let me go," Kenny growled. He fought his brother's hold, but Becca didn't think it would do him any good. Kurt had bulked up while he'd been gone and Kenny looked half his size.

"Just hold on," Kurt responded. "We can't go rushing in there. We have to get Todd out of there safely. That's the reason we're all here. To ensure that he's not hurt."

Kenny shook, but he nodded.

"Mike, Clint and I will shift. Mike and I will circle around and take the back and east side. Clint will cover the west side and Kenny and Kurt go right through the front door," RJ ordered.

Clint cracked his knuckles. "Do we get to kill them?" he asked with a little too much glee. Becca didn't know what to think about that. These guys might be a little crazy.

Kurt smacked the back of Clint's head. "No, not unless we have to."

Clint frowned. "Fine."

"Once the coast is clear, the women move in and get Todd out," RJ finished. "Go ahead and shift back, ladies."

Nikki started hers first, so Becca hurried to follow suit. Mike helped her to her feet once she was human again.

"Ready?" RJ asked.

"Yeah," Becca agreed. Nikki nodded.

"Let's go then." RJ started to shift.

"Be careful," Mike said to Becca before giving her one last kiss.

"You, too," she said with a small smile.

He drew back before transforming. Mike's change was seamless. She'd never seen anything like it, except for her father. As Alpha, he was the most powerful shifter. *Damn*. Becca was impressed.

Mike followed behind RJ. They approached at a distance, circling the old metal building. He could hear talking inside. Todd was cussing someone out. Mike wanted to laugh. He bet Carter's followers' ears were burning. Todd had some very colorful words in his vocabulary.

Once they were in position, a low whistle sounded. Kurt and Kenny were ready to enter.

Mike's muscles bunched as he prepared himself. It had been a while since he'd any action. It was wrong, but Mike was actually excited. He didn't want Todd in jeopardy, but this was fun. RJ's scent drifted from where they'd separated, so it was like old times.

There was a shout and bang as the front door was kicked open. It happened fast. Right after Kenny and Kurt made entry inside, the back door flew open and three humans ran out. RJ launched himself at them and Mike ran to help. A curse from the side of the house drew his attention as another man ran out of the back.

Mike snapped his jaw at the new man still on top of the one he'd stopped from escaping. The young, barely legal man held his hands up and froze. "Please, please don't hurt me."

He trembled and Mike smelled his fear. Mike growled and the kid pissed himself. Oh, shit, it smelt rank. Mike sneezed.

Clint came around the corner, dragging two men with him. The young man saw that and started to yell, "Please! We didn't want to do this!"

RJ crouched over the two men he had caught and snarled.

Mike nosed one closer to RJ then shifted back to human form.

The kid gasped. "Oh, God!" His eye were huge. Mike stifled a laugh.

"We won't hurt you as long as you don't run," Mike warned. "If you run, we will hunt you down."

The guy nodded. "I won't."

Mike motioned for him to join his friends on the ground. "Everyone on the ground. Put your hands behind your neck."

Mike made sure RJ and Clint had control of the prisoners before walking through the back door to join the rest of the team. Kurt was holding Owen and Barry down while Kenny stood over two humans with his hands on his hips.

Todd, Becca and Nikki stood by the front door with smiles on their faces.

Mike glanced over at Todd, who didn't look injured. He appeared to be more amused than anything else.

Todd chuckled. "My heroes," he drawled. "Did you have to wait so long to rescue me? Fuck, you were out there for hours."

The rest of the room laughed with him.

"You knew!" Kenny accused.

"Of course I did. Mike remained close by and then I picked up on your heartbeats when you joined him."

"Owen and Barry didn't?" Mike asked.

Kenny peered over at the two men in question. "I don't think they know how."

"What do you want me to do with them?" Kurt motioned to the shifters.

"Tie them up with the others. I want to talk to them one at a time," Mike said. He needed answers to ensure the threat to Becca was over.

Kurt exchanged a long look with him. Mike figured he wouldn't be doing the questioning alone.

"There's some clothes in the back room," Todd said. "Maybe everyone could stop walking around naked?"

"We'll go find them," Nikki said. She grabbed Becca's arm, drawing her from the room.

"I'll call the Alpha and inform him we've found Todd and Mike. I'll see if he wants this handled by the Pack or if he wants us to bring in the cops," Kenny said.

Clint and Mike were pushing Owen and Barry toward the kitchen.

"What are you thinking?" RJ asked, walking over to him.

Mike had to think. He needed a plan. With a nod to the front door Mike urged RJ to follow him out. He stomped down the two rickety steps before crossing to the small patch of grass. Other than the ugly, useless building, the area was nice. He stared across to the closet cluster of trees.

"You okay?" RJ asked.

"The threat to Becca won't be over until we take Carter and his entire organization down."

"I agree," RJ said.

"We have to get them to talk. No matter what it takes," Mike stated.

"I'm not keen on torturing someone in front of Nikki."

"Going soft?" Mike taunted.

"You're upset, but I'm not going to let you pick a fight with me. Save that energy for the bad guys."

Mike growled in frustration. "The humans are just scared kids. Not one of them is older than twenty-five."

"Easier to manipulate and control."

"True," Mike agreed. "So, we ask Owen or Barry."

"Owen. He's Carter's stepson."

"We need to keep the girls out of it," Mike said.

"Send them to take the humans to the Alpha."

"You're actually going to try to send us away?" Nikki shouted. She threw a pile of clothes at RJ's head. "Really?"

Becca was still standing on the porch. She was staring at Mike.

"Fuck." He rushed forward to her.

"You're going to torture them?" she asked in a whisper.

"I'm going to question them," Mike said. "We need to know where Carter is headed. More people could be a risk."

Becca pushed a pair of sweats and T-shirt into his arms. "Get dressed. I don't want anyone else seeing your bits."

Mike bristled. "Bits?"

Her smiled was forced. "Whatever you say, dear." She glanced over her shoulder toward the house. "They betrayed my dad. The entire Pack. I want them to suffer. Is that wrong?"

"No, baby," Mike assured her. "Not at all."

"I'm so angry at them."

"I know."

"We'll take the humans to my dad. You do what you have to," she said. "But you have to save a piece of them for me."

"I will," he promised.

She leaned in and kissed his cheek. "And don't take too long. I've gotten used to sleeping beside you."

Mike chuckled. They were going to be okay. "I'm sending Todd and Kenny with you."

"Of course you are," Becca said rolling her eyes.

It took too long to get Kenny, Todd, the woman, and humans on their way, RJ and Clint escorted them to Todd's SUV where the Alpha was sending more guards to meet them.

That left Mike and Kurt alone with Owen and Barry. RJ had demanded they wait for his and Clint's return before they got started.

Once the group had taken off, Mike stalked back inside.

Kurt had moved Owen and Barry into the living room. Barry was hogtied, lying on the floor in front of the couch. Owen, however, was secured to a chair that had been placed in the middle of the room. Kurt glanced up when Mike entered the room, closing the door behind him.

"We're not waiting for them to get back," Kurt guessed.

"No, we're not." He sauntered over to Owen. Kurt had done one fine job of making sure Owen didn't move. He even duct-taped his mouth. "Where'd you get the rope and duct tape?"

"Back room where the clothes were. The humans were well-stocked," Kurt said.

"Good for us," Mike stated. He crouched in front of Owen. "We're going to ask you a few questions. You're going to answer each one of them. Or I start hurting you."

Owen's voice was muffled. He squirmed and fought his holdings.

"No," Mike admonished. "I haven't asked you a question yet."

The smell of Owen's fear was so strong that it almost knocked him down. He wouldn't let any sympathy edge in, though. Owen could have killed Becca and him with the fire at her cottage. Plus the devastation in town.

"We're going to start simply," Mike said. "Where is Carter?"

Owen shook his head.

"Oh, I'm sorry." Mike ripped the duct tape from his mouth.

"Ow!" Owen spat. "Fucker."

"That's not the answer," Mike told him. "Where is Carter?"

"I don't know!" Owen shouted. "He didn't tell me. He never tells me anything."

"Oh, come on, Owen," Mike said. "He's your stepdad. He raised you as his own son. He's been here to check on you."

Owen snorted. "He hates me. He didn't come to check on me. All he wanted was a way in to the Pack. For me to find out weaknesses of the Pack."

"Was it his idea for you to join the Pack?"

Instead of answering, Owen pressed his lips into a firm line.

"Why this Pack?" Mike asked.

Owen remained quiet.

"I don't mind making you talk," Mike told him. He grinned. "I don't mind."

"I'm not talking to you." Owen had gone pale, though.

"You know," Kurt said, slamming his hand down on Owen's shoulder. "This is my pack. My entire family is still part of it. Maybe I should be the one who *talks* to him."

"We could take turns," Mike suggested.

"You think there's enough of him for both of us?" Kurt asked.

Mike glanced over his shoulder. "We still have that other guy. Maybe he feels chattier?"

"So we can kill Owen and get our info from Barry?" Kurt sounded hopeful.

"You can't kill me! I'm a cop," Owen sputtered.

This was too easy. Mike didn't think he'd even have to get his hands dirty. What a shame. "No one knows you're here, Owen. It's you and us. You think anyone cares what happens to you? If what you say is true and Carter doesn't care about you, then you've betrayed the only real family you had. The Pack would have helped you. Instead, you tried to kill the Alpha's daughter."

"I didn't want to!" Owen exclaimed. "Becca was always nice to me. As soon as my stepdad found out the council sent you here, he said we had to make an example out of you. To let the council know the war was just beginning."

"The war?" Mike repeated.

"Carter wants the shifters eradicated," Owen said.

"Even you?" Mike asked.

"Yes," Owen whispered. "It's my calling to help take out every shifter in existence then myself."

Mike exchanged a troubled look with Kurt. Holy shit, this poor kid was damaged. Mike could tell he actually believed the shit coming out of his own mouth. "What about your mom?"

"My mom?" Owen stiffened. "She doesn't have anything to do with this."

"What's she say about this plan of your stepdad's?" Mike asked.

Owen looked away. The look that flashed over his face was heartbreaking. "She says she'll pray for me."

Chapter Eight

Becca stepped out of the bathroom with a towel wrapped around her body. Mike still hadn't returned and she was growing anxious. With the immediate threat to the Pack over, Becca wasn't sure what the next steps should be. Her father had ended up calling in the local police to take custody of the humans.

She'd been by her dad's side when he'd questioned the humans. The young humans had been more than willing to talk. Becca didn't know what information Mike was getting, but the humans had been helpful. At least they now knew there wasn't a direct threat to the council.

The bedroom door opened, so she looked up. Mike paused in the threshold, staring at her.

"You okay?" she asked. He hadn't made a step into the room.

"You take my breath away."

Oh, wow, what could she say in response to that? "You like me wet from the shower? Or is it the naked part?"

He took two long strides forward before slamming the door behind him. "Technically, you're not naked. Maybe you should be."

This was a new side of him. She'd seen pieces of the dominance peeking through and could feel his power when he was shifted, but he'd been holding back on her. Her hand trembled as she gripped the top of the towel before letting it fall.

"That's better," he murmured.

His voice had deepened, sending little tendrils of desire through her body. "You like what you see?" she teased.

"I'm in a mood," he warned. "Are you sure you want to do this now? I could go take a walk to cool down."

Becca didn't want him to take a walk. She wanted to see what he could do with her. "Don't go."

"Get on your knees," he ordered.

She didn't hesitate. From her place in the middle of the room, she dropped down.

"So beautiful," he whispered, walking in a circle around her.

Once he stood in front of her, Mike yanked her T-shirt over his head. It was the same one they'd taken from the old metal building. He tossed it into the corner before sliding his thumbs into the waistband of his sweatpants.

Becca licked her lips. This was some sort of torture. All she wanted was for Mike to throw her on the floor and take her. "Please."

Mike shook his head before moving his hands to behind his back.

Damn it, she was enjoying the tease. Becca cocked her head to the side. "Are you going to stand there?"

"I might," he responded. He stood gazing at her.

Becca bit her lip. It was harder than she thought to kneel there without squirming. Mike before her in an old pair of sweats was erotic as hell.

"Close your eyes," Mike demanded.

Becca complied.

"Good. Now tip your head back."

There was a rustle of fabric and she hoped that he was finally taking off his pants. She wanted to peek.

"No peeking," he said.

She swallowed back a laugh. Mike was getting to know her pretty well.

"Now open your mouth."

Becca did so, hoping she'd get a taste of his delicious cock. There was more movement around her, but Becca wasn't going to give in and open her eyes. She wanted to enjoy this game.

Finally, after what seemed like forever, she felt the soft head of his erection caress her bottom lip. Becca stuck her tongue out, collecting the sweet juice before swallowing it. Mike groaned. She had to be patient for his next move.

"Take me all the way back." With that said, he thrust shallowly.

Becca wrapped her lips around his shaft, sucking him as deep as she could.

"That's it," he praised. "Farther."

He kept pushing in until Mike had his cock pressed to the back of her throat, making breathing difficult. Before she could pull away, he started to withdraw.

"So good. Again."

Becca had a quick moment to take a breath before he was pressing in again. The lack of oxygen, the eroticism of the moment had her head spinning. Almost literally. She didn't complain, though. Every time he removed his shaft, she would get as much air in before he shoved his erection down her throat. Each time deeper than the last.

Unable to hold back any longer, Becca opened her eyes to gaze up at him.

Mike stood with one hand tugging on his balls while he pinched his nipple with the other. She moaned. Fuck, he was so hot!

With his head thrown back, he hadn't realized that she'd disobeyed him until she made a sound.

He frowned then yanked his cock out of her mouth. "Bad girl."

Becca dropped her ass back onto her heels. "I couldn't help it."

"I guess I'll have to punish you." He held a hand out. Becca was looking forward to what he might do, so she placed her palm against his so he could lift her to her feet. Luckily, he kept his hand under her elbow, because her legs were weak. "On the bed, hands and knees. You deserve a spanking."

"Yes," she hissed. Heat burned through her body. "I've been bad."

He chuckled then helped her position the way he wanted. "If you want me to stop, all you have to say is stop. I don't ever want to hurt you."

"I want this," she told him. "Please."

"Steady yourself," he ordered.

Becca pressed her face against her folded arms.

The first smack was hard, spreading fire over her cheek and down her thigh.

She grunted.

Mike slapped the other cheek, rocking her body forward.

This time, Becca could close her eyes and feel the path the heat spread through her. She pushed her body back toward his hand. "More."

He gave it to her. Every time his hand connected with her sensitive flesh, Becca rocked back again, begging for more, the pain mixed with pleasure taking her to a high she'd never experienced before. Finally, she noticed that he'd stopped. She was almost sobbing with need by this point.

"Mike!" she called.

"That's enough," he said, gripping her hips hard. "If I don't get inside you, I'm going to explode."

"Hurry."

He climbed up on the bed, positioning himself between her legs. His skin felt cold against her, but his body was sleek with sweat as well.

"Give it to me hard and fast," she pleaded.

"Oh, I will." He slammed inside her. Becca's vision darkened as she gave her entire being over to the only man who could handle her.

* * * *

Becca rolled over in bed, reaching for Mike. After the excitement of the previous night, she was looking forward to waking next to him. When her hand found only empty bed, she sat up and searched the room. They did need to discuss waking up at the same time. She'd wanted to feel Mike's body against hers again.

In fact, her skin still tingled from the night before. She'd never been loved as hard or well before.

Mike stood at the window, watching the sun on the horizon. She wrapped the sheet around her and climbed out of bed, approaching him slowly. He didn't move when she wrapped her arms around him, kissing between his shoulder blades.

"It really is beautiful here," he said.

She hummed, pressing against his warmth. Even naked, his heat seemed to surround her. "It's even better with you here. I love my territory, but I'd been getting restless lately. I don't travel as much as I used to. Everything around me seems brighter and getting to share this place with you is awesome. There is so much more I want to show you."

He turned and gripped her shoulders. "Do you mean that?"

Becca stepped back so she could search his face. "That it's better with you here? Of course, I do. Mike" — she cupped his face between her hands — "I love having you here with me."

He closed his eyes. When he looked backed at her, she could see the hope in his gaze. "What about Kurt? If he wanted you back?"

"Mike…"

He shook his head. "I know he still has feelings for you. RJ saw it, too. I've been standing here, looking out the window, trying to decide if I could let you go if that's what you really want."

She gasped. This wasn't what she expected. Instead of basking in their lovemaking the previous night he'd been contemplating leaving her? *Oh, hell no.* Becca was not going to let him walk away. She knew how he felt about her.

He stepped away from her and started to pace. "I understand having to make hard decisions and the regrets that come with them. But you're both older now. Things have changed."

"Mike!" She didn't want Kurt any longer. She was, however, considering punching Mike.

"No." He waved his hand. "Sleeping next to you, holding you all night, and when I climbed out of bed, you reached for me. I'm not letting you go without a fight. I want you, Becca, and I'm going to do everything in my power to make sure you pick me. I thought for about five minutes that I could be the better man and step aside. I can't. If you decide it's me that you want, then I'll do everything in my power to prove to you that I'll stand by and support you."

"I already picked you!" She grabbed his hand and pulled him closer. "Not that there was a choice. Kurt and I will always be friends, but our time passed a long time ago. He's not who I see my future with."

Mike smiled. "Yeah?"

"Yes."

"We'll figure things out," Mike said. "I don't expect you to up and leave your Pack, but I can travel when you need to. Or come here. I try to stay close with my old unit since we've separated, but I want to take you to meet them."

"I'd love to," Becca said. "I already like RJ. I can't wait to see this feline Prince."

Mike laughed. "Prince Zach is cool, but his mate, Casey, is the best. He was our team leader and saved our lives numerous times. I owe him a lot."

"Then I'm sure I'll love him," Becca stated.

"We have to go to Coyote Bluff. That's where Casey's family lives. The community is a mixture of all different species of shifters, but they work together to keep their town safe. The inn is run by the best couple and the food is to die for."

Wow, as Mike grew excited about taking her to this unique place, she could feel her own eagerness grow. "Great, when do we go?"

Mike smiled. "After we know things are settled here. I don't want to leave the Pack vulnerable. Kurt and Clint are taking the shifters to the council, so they should already be gone. I know RJ is anxious to get home, too."

Becca thought about bringing up the possibility of Mike staying on with the Pack, but she wasn't sure how to broach the subject. Plus, she'd need to speak with her dad. It is the Alpha's job to pick his staff, but Becca knew that Mike would make a great addition to the Pack. "Yeah we should check in with Kenny and Todd before we leave. I think they'll be bringing their relationship out in the open. I want to support them."

"I find it hard to believe that others don't know," Mike commented. "I picked up on it the first day I was here."

"Todd was more obvious with you. It's not easy seeing a dominant wolf come in and spend time with someone you love. And Todd does love Kenny. But now that Kurt has already given his blessing, I don't think anything else will hold Kenny back. He was afraid of losing his brother's love and affection."

"Then we'll stay for a little while. Probably should finish your cottage, as well. I'm sure your dad is eventually going to want to toss me out or charge me rent if I spend much more time here," Mike said with amusement.

"I wouldn't worry about my father," Becca said. "I know how to butter him up."

Mike nodded. "He does love you."

"What about your family? You didn't mention taking me home to meet them." Becca regretted the words as soon as they came out of her mouth.

"Come sit." Mike tugged her toward the bed.

Becca wrapped the sheet tighter around her before Mike pulled her into his lap. "My unit is my family, or at least the one that I want to claim."

"But you still speak with your parents?"

"I do when I can't get out of it," he answered. "The same with my siblings. I never quite fit in with them. I was always searching for more."

"More what?"

"More than parties and social standings," Mike said. "I hate dressing up and talking Pack politics."

Becca snorted. She couldn't picture Mike in that situation. She preferred the rough and rugged side of him. "I don't blame you."

"That's all they care about, though. Power and money, I mean. My parents, especially, don't understand why I chose to serve my country, or what it means to depend on someone else for your life. I can't talk to them about what I saw. That doesn't leave us much to discuss."

"Wow, that's terrible." Becca was heartbroken. Her father had been such a positive influence and every day he made a point of saying he loved her. "What about your siblings?"

"They are my parents' perfect children. They always look the best, plus know how to make small-talk. I have nothing to offer them," Mike confessed.

"They're missing so much by not having you in their life more," Becca stated. "But I'll be more than happy to share my family with you. You'll have to take a couple of nosy aunts and crazy cousins."

"If they're a part of the package, I guess I can handle it. Plus, you haven't heard some stories about RJ and his brothers. Talk about crazy! So it's only fair."

"I don't think I'll be shocked when it comes to anything you tell me about RJ."

"Good," Mike said. "Not that I'd let you run away now that I have you."

"You have me, huh?" she teased, drawing him closer.

"Well, you are sitting on my lap." He pulled at the sheet tucked around her. "Stand up and take this off."

She rose to let it fall to the floor. Becca felt no discomfort allowing him to gaze at her so openly. Instead, she preened under his lustful look.

"So gorgeous," he praised, running his hands over her.

She arched when he cupped her breasts. "And all yours," she vowed. "So don't forget it again." She wouldn't let Mike bring up Kurt or anyone else ever again. The relationship was between the two of them.

"Yes, ma'am." He bent his head and captured one nipple in his mouth. She gasped as he tongued her, making her decide to let go of her admonishment for being cheeky. His mouth felt too damn good on her. Oh, he most surely was a breast man.

"I love your body," he said with admiration.

She hummed. That compliment wasn't something she would ever get tired of hearing. Hopefully, Mike would always look at her the way he'd been doing. She wanted to please him. There was something deep inside her that craved to submit. Becca pushed back the feeling for now, intent on enjoying.

"Come here." He led her back to the bed and gently laid her back. Mike started at her ankles and kissed his way up her legs to her thighs. She spread for him, liking where he was headed.

He peeked up at her and winked. "I'm going to show you how much I adore everything about you."

"Yes, please," she murmured.

She was already wet when he slid two fingers around her clit and teased her folds.

Becca arched up. "Please."

"We have time, baby." He teased with his fingers again.

She didn't care if they had the rest of their lives. She wanted to be filled. "Mike…"

He chuckled. "So impatient." He lowered his head and used his tongue to enter her.

"Oh, God!" she cried.

"Taste so good."

"Feels good," she responded.

He added two fingers while she pressed closer. But it wasn't enough. "Mike, please."

He lifted his head. "More?"

She dropped her head back. "Please!"

He chuckled but moved up her body. Thankfully, he continued to thrust his fingers inside. His mouth covered hers and she opened for him while riding his hand.

He pulled away panting. "Mine," he declared.

"Yes, yes."

Removing his fingers, he climbed over her, his cock pushing at her entrance. "Mine!"

The possessiveness was enough to almost send her over the edge.

"Yes! Mike."

He slammed inside as she called out his name over and over. He rode her fast and hard.

She loved every second of it.

Becca gripped his shoulders, nails digging in, and growled, "You're mine, too."

Mike plunged in hard and stilled. "That's right, baby." He pulled out and flipped her over.

She climbed on her hands and knees and raised her ass back at him. He gripped her hips and this time entered her slowly. She tried to push back and get him inside faster, but his hold was too strong.

"No, you take what I give you," he ordered.

He slid out before pushing back in. It was such good torture.

She squeezed her inner muscles, clamping down on his cock.

"Oh, baby," he groaned.

She threw her head back. "Harder."

Obviously at the end of his control, he pumped into her quickly. She met every thrust and urged him on. He reached around, rubbing her clit as he pounded inside.

She exploded, tightening around him.

"Becca!" he moaned, slammed.

"I'm not done with you," he promised.

Becca laid her forehead in her arms. The bed rocked under the motion while her body remained relaxed.

Mike's thrusts grew erratic and it didn't take long for him to grunt then come.

They collapsed on the bed together, sweaty and exhausted.

"Well, glad we got that talk out of the way," Becca said, laughing.

He smacked her ass. "Be nice."

"Oh, I'm always nice," she teased.

He pulled out then helped her to roll onto her back. Becca threw her leg over his before wrapping an arm around his chest.

"We should get up for breakfast," she murmured.

"In a minute," he said. "I want to enjoy holding you for a minute."

"Speaking of holding," she said. "Just once, we need to wake up in bed at the same time. I was cold."

"Tomorrow," he declared. "Or maybe later today if we can sneak in a nap."

"I like naps," she approved. "Especially if they're with you."

Mike was starving by the time he and Becca left the bedroom. They made it to the kitchen as breakfast was ending. Nikki and RJ appeared to have only sat down, too. Mike slapped RJ on the back as he passed then took a seat next to him. Becca grabbed the coffee pot to fill mugs and one of the women still cooking pointed at the dishes.

"Eat up now! You deserve a good treat," she said.

"Yes, ma'am," RJ and Mike said at the same time.

Plates were filled and bowls passed around. Kenny and Todd came in the back door holding hands. That was good to see. Sure, most of the people in the room already knew about them, but small steps would eventually lead to more.

Mike liked the couple so hopefully there were no bigots inside the Pack. He didn't see Alpha Nelson putting up with that bullshit. The Alpha appeared to be a very open-minded and loving leader.

"See, I told you we didn't miss breakfast." Todd pushed Kenny out of the way and grabbing his own plate.

Kenny rolled his eyes but continued to watch Todd with a fond expression in his eyes.

The women set the last of the food on the table and removed their aprons. Mike waited until the ladies left before speaking.

"How're you doing?" he asked Todd.

Todd grinned. "I'm all right. They didn't hurt me. They were more scared of me than anything. I had some fun of my own flashing my fangs."

"He couldn't let us rescue his ass," Kenny complained. "I was working on my white-knight look and everything."

Todd patted Kenny on the back. "Next time I get kidnapped, I'll make sure to be suitably scared and cower down before the big, bad humans. Then you can swoop in and rescue the damsel in distress. "

Kenny growled. "I don't swoop."

"And he's no damsel," Becca said. "I should get that title, damn it."

"No kidnapping for you." Mike pointed his finger at her. He knew everyone was joking, but the thought of Becca being taken filled him with cold dread.

"Yes, dear," Becca replied. "Besides, all the bad guys should be out of town by now."

"Did Kurt leave with Owen and Barry this morning?" RJ questioned.

Kenny nodded. "Left at sunrise. The council wants to talk to them about the connection with Dan Carter."

Todd snorted. "That man is bat-shit crazy. Going on about how I was the spawn of the devil. Had all the humans in there too scared to even touch me. As if I could turn them by looking into their eyes."

"Is he going to be arrested?" Nikki inquired.

Kenny sighed. "I spoke with the sheriff this morning. While the men he arrested last night are scared, they still claim that Dan Carter was never there and it was all their idea to kidnap Todd. The sheriff thinks they are more afraid of Carter than doing jail time."

"That doesn't even make sense," Becca complained.

Kenny shrugged. "They'll open an investigation, but without proof it'll be tough."

"But Todd saw him," Becca argued.

"It's Todd's word against eight humans and two other wolves," Kenny maintained. "They'll push for a better confession and try to tie him in."

"That's not his biggest problem, anyway," RJ stated.

Everyone turned to him.

"Word's out to all the Packs. Plus, the council is already investigating him on their own. He won't get so close the next time. He lost the element of surprise," RJ continued.

"Good," Becca said. "No one else should have to go through all of this."

"But that also means we don't know how he'll approach the next Pack," RJ said. "Instead of setting fires to draw anyone out, he might go for a shifter who doesn't suspect he's around."

"Oh." Becca glanced at Mike.

He covered her hand with his. "The council will do what they can. Let's let them worry about other places and concentrate on your Pack."

"Like Barry and Owen betraying us?"

"So what was Barry's connection? I can understand Owen, but Barry?" Mike asked.

Kenny and Todd shook their heads.

"Could it be as simple as Barry being friends with Owen?" Becca asked.

"But to turn on his own Pack?" Kenny asked.

"I overheard him talking to Owen about you, Becca."

"What did he say?" Mike demanded. Fuck, why hadn't he been told that earlier?

"Just how wrong it is that she's dating someone from another Pack. As the Alpha's daughter, her bloodline should stay pure and only those inside our Pack should have a chance with her."

"Someone like Barry?" Mike snorted. "He's not a strong enough shifter or man to be Becca's type."

Becca looked at him before lifting a brow.

"What?" Mike asked. "It's true and you know it."

"He might not be my type—"

"Totally not your type," Mike interrupted.

"Not at all," Kenny added.

"You'd eat him alive," Todd added.

Becca threw up her hands. "So not the point!"

"Actually, I think that was completely the point," RJ interjected.

"Fine," she conceded. "But that was still no reason to turn on us."

"It's not," Kenny said. "But I don't think Barry was all together there, anyway. Why else would he side with the humans? He's a fucking shifter. They'd have eventually killed him, too."

"Not a smart man," RJ stated.

"I'm glad it's over," Todd said.

Kenny leaned into Todd's shoulder.

Becca smiled at the couple.

"Yeah, yeah, yeah," Kenny said. "We spoke to the Alpha last night—we're done hiding our relationship. We have his support, the support of our friends and family, so I asked Todd to mate with me."

The table exploded in congratulations and cheering.

Todd was grinning. "Finally getting a commitment from him," he teased.

"That is so great! But what about your position? Did you make a decision on that?" Becca asked. "I thought you didn't want to be away from Todd as much once you mated."

"Wait. What?" Todd turned to Kenny. "You spoke to Becca about mating me?"

"I told you last night I wasn't asking you spur of the moment. Yes, I spoke to Becca about it. Made plans. It's something I've always wanted to do. I was chickenshit," Kenny told him.

Todd nuzzled Kenny's neck while whispering something into his ear. Mike was glad he couldn't hear what was said when Kenny started wiggling in his chair.

"Later, babe," Kenny murmured to Todd.

Todd laughed.

"As for my position?" Kenny shrugged. "If someone wants to challenge me, I'll have to deal with it then. If I think the shifter will be good enough, I'll step down. If not, I'll fight to hold on to it. Besides, I'm hoping maybe sometime soon I can pass it on by picking my own replacement. Let me concentrate on my fire training."

Kenny caught Mike's gaze and held it. Mike understood what he meant. Todd had already put the thought in his head. Mike wasn't sure he wanted to get so deep so soon. It was something he'd think about, but not make any decisions as of yet.

He smiled to let Kenny know he understood the message.

RJ stretched his arm behind Nikki's shoulder, drawing his attention. RJ smirked and Mike knew he had also caught what Kenny wasn't saying.

"So, Mike, what's next for you?" his friend asked, pretending innocence.

Mike laughed. "Nice, man." But he wasn't upset. Kenny was pretty obvious as it was. He twined his fingers with Becca's. "Right now, I'll be staying with Becca. We need to see about rebuilding her house. Plus, I want to take her to meet the rest of the unit. I might even travel up to introduce her to the Cross brothers, but only if Nikki promises to leash you."

"Ha!" RJ pointed at him. "You act all innocent now, but the last wrestling match I remember was you and Dylan. I believe the coffee table was the casualty of that one."

"It was," Nikki piped up.

"Whatever." Mike waved them away. "Once we're sure things are good here, we'll try to see everyone."

"Oh, I was going to talk to you about something," RJ jumped up. "Come on!"

The change was so sudden that Mike didn't react for several moments. Nikki actually had to nudge him.

"He's like a toddler," Nikki commented. "He thinks of something and nothing else matters." She pointed toward the back door RJ had already exited. "Don't think he won't return and drag your ass out with him."

Mike gazed down at his half-eaten plate. Damn it, he was still hungry. "Fine." He dropped his napkin next to his plate before he rose. He dropped a kiss on Becca's temple before striding across the room. RJ stood in the middle of the yard with his hands on his hips.

"What took you so long?" RJ called.

Mike closed the sliding glass door behind him before walking to his friend. "I was eating," he complained.

"Okay, don't be mad," RJ told him.

Well shit, that meant he was about to be pissed off. "What did you do?"

"I was only trying to help."

"Which is when we usually find ourselves with bullets aimed at our heads."

"It's not that bad," RJ exclaimed. "I just made some phone calls."

"Some? To who?"

"And I didn't know you wanted to travel with Becca. So, really this is your fault for not telling me."

"I don't even know what you're talking about," Mike griped.

"I knew you'd want to have Becca's place fixed up quickly. You can't like having her dad down the hall when you're—"

"I get the idea," Mike stated. He didn't want to hear RJ try to explain what he did with Becca behind closed doors. There is no telling what would come out of RJ's mouth.

"So, I called in help."

Mike understood. And he had a bad feeling about what RJ meant. "Who did you call?"

"Everyone."

"You did what?" Mike wanted to strangle his friend.

"If we all pitch in, it won't hardly take any time at all," RJ defended. "I wanted to help."

"And it didn't occur to you that having Becca meet everyone, all at once, might be a little too much?"

"I asked Alpha Nelson," RJ said. "He thought it was a great idea."

"Of course he did! He doesn't have to worry about scaring her off."

"We won't scare her off." RJ looked affronted. "I mean, we're not that bad."

"Claude threatened to burn his entire inn down if we all came back at the same time ever again," Mike reminded him.

"Oh, yeah." RJ frowned. "I'm sure it'll be fine this time, though."

Mike couldn't believe this. "I'm going to kill you."

RJ danced back. "Really? You think you can catch me?"

"I'm not playing RJ." He couldn't keep a damn smile off his face, though. It didn't matter how much RJ pissed him off—Mike knew his friend had only been trying to help.

"Come on! You probably are out of practice. You've been slacking in your training. Casey is going to be so disappointed."

"I have not been slacking in my training!" Mike exclaimed.

"I don't know, man." RJ swiped at him. "You've been moving pretty slow."

The next time RJ swung, Mike caught his arm. In a practiced move, he yanked, throwing RJ off-balance. Mike should have anticipated RJ kicking out the back of his knee.

Both of them hit the ground hard. RJ was already trying to roll him onto to his stomach. Mike dug his heels in before bashing his forehead into RJ's.

"Fuck!" RJ spat. "I hate when you do that. It hurts."

Mike wrapped his arm around RJ's neck. "I know. That's why I do it."

They wrestled for a few more minutes, each getting the upper hand before the other countered the move. Mike hadn't realized how much he'd missed goofing off.

"I knew they'd end up covered in dirt, grass and blood," Nikki commented.

"Oh, shit!" RJ whispered. "Busted."

Mike glanced onto the back porch and saw both Nikki and Becca standing there. "He started it." He pointed at RJ.

"I did not!" RJ slapped his hand away.

"Did, too," Mike argued.

"Jeez, really, guys?" Nikki complained. "You're not a couple of four year olds."

"Hey, Mike," Becca called.

Mike was still pinned halfway under RJ. "Yes, Becca?"

"Dad asked Kenny to get some of the guest cottages ready for some of your friends. Would you like to tell me what's going on? Or are you having too much fun playing with your friend?" Becca asked.

RJ started to laugh so Mike elbowed her in the ribs.

RJ grunted, giving Mike the opportunity to slip out from under him.

Mike stood, making a production of dusting off his clothes before turning back to Becca. "I want you to remember my next words. Repeat them several times, okay?"

Becca frowned. "Okay."

"This is all RJ's fault."

"What?"

"No," Mike said. "Repeat, this is all RJ's fault."

"Why?"

"Because it is. It always is," Mike told her. "This is all RJ's fault."

"This is all RJ's fault," she repeated.

"Good." Mike strode forward. "Just remember, I warned you."

Chapter Nine

The guest cottages were ready by the time the first of Mike's friends arrived. Becca was both nervous and anxious to meet the people Mike considered his real family.

"You ready for this?" Nikki came up behind her. They were standing in the middle of the backyard getting ready for the impromptu barbecue to welcome everyone. Mike, RJ, Todd and Kenny had run into town to pick up the lumber and sheetrock that her father had ordered.

"No," Becca confessed. "This is crazy."

"Well, look on the bright side," Nikki suggested. "You get this all out of the way at once."

"Yeah, great," she muttered.

"It probably won't help that my brothers will be here, as well. Brandon and RJ have this love–hate thing going on."

"I like Brandon," Becca said.

"Just don't like him more than RJ or I'll deal with a pouting mate until we leave."

Becca had to smile. The relationship these friends had made her appreciate her own. Todd and Kenny were as special to her as Mike's group was to him. They weren't as colorful.

"I don't pout."

Both woman squealed and jumped as RJ spoke behind them. Becca whirled around to glare at him.

"And no one likes Brandon more than me," RJ claimed.

Becca squinted at him. "Are you sure? Maybe we should take a poll."

"God, please don't encourage this feud between them," Mike said, joining them. He automatically put his arm around her shoulder. Becca leaned into him. "They're both infuriating."

"I resent that," RJ stated. He spun on Nikki. "And you have to stop taking your brother's side. I don't care if he raised you. You are my mate! I'm always right."

"Except when you argue with me," Nikki replied.

"Or me," Mike said.

"Especially me."

Becca's head was spinning. Mike turned her toward the new voice and she almost swallowed her tongue. Two gorgeous men stood in front of them holding hands.

"Casey. Zachary," Mike greeted. "You made good time."

"Because he drives like a hell cat," the taller of the two said.

"Forgive Zach," Casey, or who Becca assumed was Casey, said. "He doesn't appreciate my fine motor skills."

"I appreciate all your skills, my love. You just don't have any when it comes to driving."

"It's true," RJ said. "Casey rolled over more vehicles than anyone else in the unit."

"You came in a close second," Casey told RJ.

Mike laughed before bending to whisper into Becca's ear, "He is the most mature out of all of us. Now I'm questioning the rest of our sanity."

"I heard that," Casey exclaimed. "And come greet me properly before introducing me to your girl."

Mike stepped forward, but Casey was already rushing to grab him and lift him into a bear hug. Mike grunted, beating on Casey's back, and Casey chuckled manically. Finally, after several long minutes, Casey dropped Mike back down to his feet.

"Damn, man," Mike complained. "Do you ever stop working out?"

"Of course not." He pointed toward Zach. "People keep trying to kidnap my man."

Zach stepped forward, holding out his hand. "Nice to see you again, Mike."

"You, too." In a much more civilized manner, Zach and Mike greeted each other. "I'd also like to meet your lady."

"Yeah? Who told you?" Mike asked. "I would have liked to tell everyone myself."

"Who do you think?" Casey replied.

Everyone looked at RJ.

"What?" RJ threw his hands up. "Of course, I told. No one is surprised."

Becca didn't know what to make of the introductions to the feline Prince and his mate. This was not how she expected the interaction to take place. She found herself smiling, even though she was still nervous.

"Okay," Mike said. "Zachary, you're the most normal one here. I'd like to introduce you to Becca." With a firm hand on her lower back, Mike urged her forward.

"It's very nice to meet you, Becca," Zachary shook her hand. "I've spoken to your father several times and can see why he speaks so highly of you." He bent his head to kiss the top of her hand. "It's a true pleasure."

Becca shuddered. She might be falling hard for Mike, but Zachary was a whole other level of smooth. His deep voice sent tingles down her spine.

"Good, isn't he?" Casey asked Mike while Mike frowned. "This is what I put up with."

"Okay, never mind." Mike retook her hand from Zachary. "You don't get to talk to Zach."

Zachary chuckled then winked at her. Yeah, the Prince was screwing with Mike.

"This is my old team leader and Zachary's mate, Casey." Mike motioned. "He's almost as bad as RJ, so don't believe anything he says about me."

"Hey!" Casey smacked Mike. "Be nice. I still know how to take you down."

Mike rolled his eyes. "Where's your shadow, Zachary?"

Casey snorted. "Craig met a girl. He'd already committed to meeting her parents this weekend, or he would have been here. Actually, he tried to get out of his obligations by using you as an excuse, but Zach finally made him go," Casey said.

"He'd canceled three times already," Zachary stated. "Luna's parents were going to think she'd made him up."

"Oh, wow." Mike glanced at her. "Craig is Zachary's personal bodyguard. I thought he stayed in the room when they — "

"Mike," Casey growled out a warning.

"What?" Mike laughed. "That's what RJ told me."

Becca couldn't hold back any longer. She laughed, leaning into Mike to hold her up. Oh, this was going to be fun. She hadn't needed to worry. Mike's friends — his family, really — were awesome.

"Let the party begin!"

"Brandon!" Nikki rushed over to her older brother.

"Hey, squirt," Brandon said before lifting her off her feet to swing her around.

"Put me down, you big lump," Nikki complained.

Brandon merely hugged her tighter. Becca already knew Nikki's brothers Brandon and Justin, as well as the man she held hands with. Ben was RJ's younger brother and she'd met him at the mating ceremony. She greeted everyone before looking around. Spotting Kyle and Todd hovering by the back door, she waved them over. It was time to mix her own bit of crazy in with the group.

Mike bent down to pull a couple of beers out of the ice chest before straightening up to peer over the yard. Thanks to Becca's father and Pack, the cleanup had already been done on Becca's cottage before his friends had arrived. That had helped with planning on where to begin.

Casey had worked with Becca to design the changes she wanted to bring in while informing her of what would need to be replaced. Mike had no idea that his former leader had experience and talent in construction. He was impressed.

Mike was also shocked that the damage wasn't as bad as it had first appeared. With the debris cleared away, they were actually making progress. And it had only been a few days.

"It's going well."

Mike handed RJ one of the bottles as his best friend joined him. "Yeah," he agreed. "At this rate, Becca will be moved back in about a week."

"Which means the two of you can be out of the Alpha house." RJ fake shuddered. "I can't imagine you have any fun being under the Alpha's roof."

Thinking back on what he and Becca had gotten up to, Mike could only grin. When he was with Becca, it didn't matter where they were—he couldn't keep his hands off her body.

"Really?" RJ thumped him on the back. "You dog."

Mike punched RJ in the leg. "*Dog?*"

"Woof. Woof."

"I swear, I don't see how Nikki puts up with you," Mike said.

"Hey! She loves me just the way I am. You've been my best friend longer," RJ pointed out. "What's that say about you?"

"You're right," Mike said. "I need to have my head examined."

"Nah," RJ told him. "You're my brother from another mother."

Mike groaned.

"Speaking of mothers, yours called."

"What?" Mike jerked away. He was having a great day. The last thing he wanted to think about was his family.

"Ben has been watching my shop for me while I've been gone," RJ explained. "I guess you haven't been answering the phone, so your mom called my place this morning. Ben told her that we were both out of town, but he didn't know whether she believed him or cared. She told him to let you know that you're expected home next week. There is some big event she wants you to attend."

Mike snorted. "Yeah, right."

"I don't know, man, from what Ben told me, she's pretty insistent."

Of course, she was. It didn't matter what Mike had going on in his life. His parents expected him to jump whenever they said. He wasn't going to do it this time, though. Mike had responsibilities here and he wouldn't let Becca down. "They'll have to manage without me."

RJ snorted. "I know the others don't know about your family, but this is me you're talking to." RJ grabbed his arm before pulling him farther from the others. When he turned Mike to look at him, RJ was frowning. "You know the shit your mom will pull if you ignore her. Hell, you being halfway around the world didn't keep her off your back."

Mike sighed. After one intense mission, his commander had tracked him down to inform him that his mother had called his office every single day. While his commander refused to give his mom any information on his whereabouts, he'd been frustrated by the way Mike's mother had acted.

After a huge blow-up with his parents when he'd finally arrived back in the States, they'd backed off, for about two months. Now it appeared they'd forgotten the promises they'd made. Mike would return home when he was able. Not at their command. "I can handle them."

RJ snorted. "They'll love Becca."

"They're not going to meet her."

"Yeah, right," RJ scoffed. "I hate to tell you this, Mike, but you're already falling in love with Becca. I know how that goes. You're not going to want to leave her. Not even to visit your parents."

"I'll make it a quick weekend trip when I get time," Mike responded.

RJ shook his head. "No, you won't."

Mike threw his arms up in the air. "What do you want me to do?"

"Admit how you feel," RJ replied. "Don't lose the best thing that ever happened to you."

"I don't plan on it," Mike snapped.

"So you're staying here?"

"I…I haven't—"

"Because Becca is never going to leave her Pack, her father."

"I know that."

"I can see you'd fit in here," RJ said. "They need a strong solider who'll put himself in the line of danger."

"You don't think this is over?" Mike had only been concerned about getting Becca back in her home and where they'd go from there.

"I don't think Dan Carter will be the only one who targets this Pack," RJ stated. "They're going to need help, lots of it."

Mike turned so he could take in his friends, Becca's family, and other Pack members who were spending hours to rebuild a home. They were taking time from their own lives to help someone else. They didn't have to, but this was what family did. "I won't let anything happen to them," Mike promised.

"Then you're staying?" RJ was behind him.

From where they stood, both men had a direct line of sight to where Becca and Nikki stood sanding down a few of the new porch steps. "I'm staying."

As the words left his mouth, Becca lifted her head to peer at him. There was no way that she'd heard him, but as their gazes met, she grinned at him. God, he wasn't going to be able to leave her. RJ was right. He would be by Becca's side all the time. She was everything he didn't know he'd wanted.

* * * *

"I don't think it takes four people to place a lumber order," Mike bitched as he drove through town.

Beside him RJ chuckled. "We're picking up pizza, too. And beer."

"Becca and I could have handled it," Mike told him.

"Yes, but I'm hungry," RJ whined. "That means we don't have time for you to park and get some alone time."

Mike glanced into the rearview mirror to look at Becca. She gazed back with a smile. That had been exactly their plan.

"Besides," RJ said, "Brandon was getting on my nerves."

Nikki snorted. "You were the one baiting him."

"It's just so easy," RJ said. "He always acts like he's so smart."

"Because he is," Mike taunted. "He's had your number since day one."

"He's pissed because I'm sleeping with his sister."

"Hey!" Nikki smacked RJ.

"No, he couldn't stand you before that," Mike pointed out.

"I don't think you're helping," Becca said.

Mike laughed.

"This is payback." RJ shrugged. "Mike thinks he's funny, but in reality, he knows I'm always right."

He scoffed. RJ might be his best friend and the person he trusted the most, but he was definitely not always right.

"Pull over," RJ demanded in a hard voice as he sat up straight in his seat.

Mike didn't hesitate. He jerked the steering wheel to the right while slamming on the brakes. They skidded to a stop. "What's wrong?"

"Look." He nodded ahead of them on the road.

He squinted through the windshield at the two big black SUVs blocking the street. "What the hell?" he muttered.

"What's going on?" Becca peered between the front seats.

"You and Nikki stay in the car," Mike ordered. He unbuckled his seatbelt before glancing over at RJ. RJ nodded in return.

"Excuse me?" Nikki spat. "We're not staying in the car."

"Yes, you are," RJ demanded.

"Please." Mike held up a hand when he saw Nikki starting to argue. "We might need to make a quick exit."

Nikki huffed. "Fine."

Mike turned to Becca. "If RJ and I start to shift, you get behind this wheel and take off. This might be an attack against you and the Pack. You'll have to warn your dad."

Becca held up her phone. "I will. be careful."

RJ laughed. "We're trained for this. It's about time we had some real fun."

Nikki shook her head. "Hurry up and deal with this. I want my damn pizza."

"And beer," Mike added.

"Yes, beer," Becca murmured. "Lots and lots of beer."

Mike offered her a confident smile. "It'll be okay."

She nodded.

He reached for the door handle, taking deep breaths. The hairs on his arms were standing up with his unease. There was no reason anyone should be out in the dark blocking them from town. Only people from the Pack would drive this direction.

Mike and RJ came together in front of their own vehicle and stood tall. Experience and knowing what RJ would do in most situations would see them through whatever they'd battle.

"Can you smell anything?" RJ questioned.

"No, they're too far away."

"I don't like this," RJ said. "They can't know it would be us coming down this road."

"Just stay ready," Mike warned.

Several doors opened, but it was the man who'd exited from the farther SUV's back seat who had his attention.

"Dan Carter," he spat.

Beside him, RJ was growling. Mike was glad his best friend was with him. RJ might be a little crazy, but he'd make sure Mike didn't do anything stupid.

Carter strolled with a cocky stride, stopping about a dozen feet from him.

"I got your back," RJ whispered.

"Keep an eye on the girls," Mike said. "This could be a trap to get Becca."

"No one will get past me," RJ promised.

Mike stalked forward. He made certain that he stared Carter in the eye the entire time.

"Mike Jackson," Carter said. "I was hoping it would be you who left that property first."

"Something you need?" Mike asked. "If not, why don't you get your vehicles out of the fucking road? You're in my way."

Carter sneered. "I'd like you to give a message to the other creatures like you."

Mike didn't snarl. Instead he let his fangs drop and gave his toothiest grin.

Carter's arrogant façade faltered. As close as Mike was, he could smell the man's fear. *Good, Carter should be scared of me.*

"Be careful with your words," Mike suggested. "The police are already searching for you. You don't want to add any more problems to your load."

"If the police are going to side with animals, then they will no longer be able to hold positions of authority. Times are changing," Carter stated.

"They are," Mike agreed. He took two steps forward. The sweat gathered at Carter's temples. "You won't get away with hurting people."

"People?" Carter repeated. "You're an animal."

"No, that's you, attacking a town that never did anything to you."

"Yet. How long until your kind decides you should rule over us? Make us your slaves?"

"We don't want slaves. We want to live our lives out in the open."

"It doesn't matter what you say. I'm giving you a warning to pass along. Do with it what you want," Carter said.

"Go ahead." Mike crossed his arms over his chest. He let the muscles flex to show Carter he had more than one way to hurt him.

"Hide," Carter threatened. "Run and hide. Anyone left will be taken out like the animals they are."

Mike did snarl this time. "Who are you to threaten us?"

"I'm the man, the human, who will shoot you myself."

Mike lunged, but Carter was pulled back by one of his men and a gun was pointed at Mike's head. Behind him, RJ growled.

"You'll see me again," Carter warned.

It took everything in him not to attack. If Becca hadn't been close enough for a stray bullet to hit her, Mike would have taken Carter down. It was hard to let Carter walk away. He didn't deserve to be free. Mike would track him down, though.

Carter climbed back in the SUV before his men walked slowly backward to join him. Mike kept his sharp teeth. He wanted to shift completely but that would leave him vulnerable.

He didn't take his eye off the threat until the two SUVs backed away and drove off. Only then did he turn to RJ.

His best friend was pissed. RJ's eyes were glowing and his fangs showed, as well.

"Mike!"

The back doors flew open as both Becca and Nikki raced toward them.

"Are you okay?" Becca launched herself into his arms.

"Shh," he soothed. She was trembling.

"When I saw that gun at your head, I thought I was going to lose control. I almost shifted," she whispered.

"I'm okay," he assured her. Mike looked over her head at RJ and Nikki. Nikki appeared pissed as RJ spoke quietly to her. "It's all going to be okay."

She pulled back. "It's not over. Even after all of this they're going to keep coming after us."

Becca was right. Mike needed to talk to the council. There was going to be trouble coming to all the shifters. "I'm not going anywhere. We're going to take care of your family. I promise."

She lay her cheek against his chest. "I believe you."

"Good," Mike told her. "Let's get our errands done. We need to contact your dad and the council."

"Okay." She gripped his hand tightly as they walked back to the vehicle.

Mike nodded to the driver's side. "You mind?" he asked RJ.

"No problem." RJ redirected Nikki to the seat behind him.

Mike helped Becca settle in before reaching for her phone. "I need to talk to your dad."

"Sure." She pressed her cell into his palm. "I had him on the phone as you spoke to Carter. We heard most of it. I told him I'd call him back once Carter left."

As RJ got them back on the way, Mike pressed the most recent call on Becca's phone.

"Becca? Are you all okay?" Alpha Nelson said in greeting.

"It's Mike. Carter's gone. No one was hurt."

"I called the police. I'm hoping they can pick him up, but I doubt it. Carter would know we'd try to get him arrested. I'm sure he had an escape plan without being seen."

"I agree," Mike said. "We need to tell the others. I think he'll leave us alone for a while and target someone else."

"Are you sure?"

"Yes. But he may leave some of his followers behind. Since he's wanted, I expect him to already be gone."

The Alpha sighed. "It seems we'll be on high alert for a long time. At least until Carter and the other humans like him get caught."

"Carter is truly afraid. I know the council worked with some of the other shifters to come out. We need to get the word out to everyone. Zach can help with the felines," Mike replied.

"I tried to keep our troubles out of the media so we didn't lose the tourism business. Our town relies on that to survive."

"I understand and don't blame you."

"Maybe it wasn't the right move."

Mike turned to look at Becca and Nikki in the back seat. "Actually, that was smart. Now you can decide how and what comes out."

"You have a plan?" Alpha Nelson asked.

Becca glanced up at him and nodded. As shifters, everyone in the car was able to hear both sides of the conversation. "Yes, I think I know what to do. We'll have the details worked out by the time we get back."

"Do you want me to send Kenny and Todd out to meet you? I don't like the four of you being on your own."

"Probably best to keep everyone else away from town until we know Carter is gone for good."

"Okay, hurry back. And watch over my girl."

"I promise." Mike hung up. He passed the phone back to Becca.

"What do you want us to do?" Becca asked.

"We're going to use some of those devastating photos of yours before taking some more."

"You want us to tell everyone what happened?" Nikki asked.

"No," Mike replied. "We're going to show everyone how we're rebuilding. Instead of leading with fear, we're going to be positive and show the humans they won't win. The Packs will stand together."

Becca smiled. "I like that."

Chapter Ten

Becca rubbed her eyes before pushing away from her laptop. She'd released her third article on an online forum. So far, her other two had already been picked up by major news stations. Nikki's own write-ups had even been selected by some international sites.

"Tired?" Mike came up behind her and rubbed her shoulders. She leaned back, grateful to feel his hands on her. The stress of having bringing Carter's actions to the attention of the world was exhausting. She was even having trouble sleeping, having to relive the horror of the fires. What could have happened, people dying, or being seriously hurt, bothered her more than Becca wanted to admit to anyone. She felt a ton of responsibility weighing her down.

"Yes, at least we're making a difference," she said.

"Better than I'd even thought," Mike said. "It's good see how many humans on actually on our side. If nothing else comes from this, we now know we have support."

"But it's been five days and we still haven't heard a word about Dan Carter. He can't get away with what he did here."

"He won't," Mike promised. "It's not only the local police here looking for him. With what you and Nikki have done, his picture is out there everywhere. There's not going to be anywhere he can hide."

"I hope not," she stated.

"Come upstairs with me. I'll give you a full body massage." Mike urged her to her feet. "And more."

Becca almost melted against him. As busy as they'd been, she missed spending real time with Mike. Between meetings he was involved in, her work, and rebuilding the cottage, by the time they went to bed, they were both exhausted. Not that they hadn't made love every night, but she missed Mike's lingering touches.

The Alpha house was quiet around them, everyone else except for her father had already gone to bed. She could faintly hear her dad's voice in his office where he must have been on the phone. It seemed all her father did these days was spend time making calls to other Packs and the council.

"We'll be able to finish up your house tomorrow. Are you excited to be able to move back in?" Mike asked.

"I really am," Becca admitted. "It feels like that's the first step of putting everything behind us."

"True." Mike opened the bedroom door before nudging her inside. "Go lie down. I'm going to grab some stuff from the bathroom."

Becca nodded before walking to the bed. She started to undress at the end of the mattress, tossing her clothes onto the chair located in the corner. Once she was naked, she crawled up and settled with Mike's pillow under her head. She wanted to be able to smell him. His natural musk was such a turn-on.

She closed her eyes as Mike did whatever it was he needed in the bathroom. She didn't care as long as he returned soon.

"You are so beautiful," he murmured from somewhere over her shoulder.

"I'm all yours." She didn't even lift her head. It was getting easier saying the words. Becca didn't want to pressure Mike into a relationship that he might not be ready for, but she couldn't imagine not seeing him every day.

The mattress dipped and his knees brushed against her sides. She didn't open her eyes, relaxed farther into the bed. When he straddled her legs, she wiggled in a tease.

"Stop that!" he chided. A quick, gentle tap on her ass followed his words. "I want to take care of you."

"You always do," she told him.

"Shh." Mike brushed a kiss at the nape of her neck. Instead of relaxing, Becca was thinking about rolling onto her back and seducing him into riding her hard.

"Just let me touch you," he urged, sinking his fingers into the tense knuckles of her shoulders.

There was no way that she could hold in the low, long groan. His touch felt great.

Mike continued to manipulate her muscles until she was a barely able to lift her head. Becca had no idea how long he worked but had started to drift off when he stopped. She moaned in protest.

"Roll over onto your back," he commanded.

It took a lot of effort to comply, but when Mike lifted himself off her legs, she managed to twist around until she could flop and sprawl.

"You look completely melted," he commented, settling back down. His erection brushed over her thigh. He only wore a loose pair of sweatpants.

"I am," she murmured. "I don't want to ever move again."

"Well, then…" Mike dropped down with his mouth hovering over her stomach. "Let's test that theory, shall we?"

Mike ran his tongue in a circle around her belly button. Becca gasped. She shivered, surprised when her body actually began to respond.

"How's this feel?" he asked, before trailing his lips lower following an unhidden path toward where she wanted to feel his mouth.

Becca clutched at the back of his head, hoping to guide him.

"I thought you were too tired to move," he teased.

"Mike!" she whined.

He slipped a finger through her slick folds until he teased at the entrance of her pussy. She bent her knees while pulling her legs up. Becca opened for him.

"I want to taste you," he murmured.

"Yes," she hissed.

Mike licked up the path of her inner thigh. Becca trembled. Then he was running his tongue over her clit. Becca tensed before clutching at the back of his head.

The flat of his tongue opened her and Becca arched, unable to resist. A finger joined Mike's tongue until Becca was pushing against him. Sweat began to trickle from her hairline with the way that fire consumed her.

Eventually, she had to push at Mike's shoulders. "I want you inside me."

He leaned back on his heels. "Roll over."

This time, Becca had no problem complying. She flipped before raising onto her hands and knees. Mike's hand was gentle as he palmed her ass cheeks.

"I'll never get tired of looking at your body," he said.

Becca rocked back until she felt his cock brush her entrance. "I hope you don't." She wasn't sure if the passion would always be consuming between them, but she could hope.

Mike gripped one hip hard, his fingers digging in, then the tip of his shaft was pressing in.

There was no pain, a feeling of rightness that he was filling her. Mike's thick cock was all she could think about. The earlier issues, stress and worries floated away until all Becca cared about was where Mike was connecting them.

He thrust hard and deep, rocking the bed.

Becca cried out in pure pleasure.

"You belong to me," Mike said. His voice was low, barely audible, but the words still echoed around in her head. The claim spoke to a part of her shared by her wolf.

She tightened her inner muscles around his shaft, drawing out a desperate moan from him. "Mine," she called back.

Mike started a rhythm that she could barely keep up with. Each plunge was deeper and harder than the last. The constant sound that escaped from her mouth rose in volume.

When her orgasm was ripped out of her, she buried her face in the pillow to muffle the scream. Mike fucked her through the climax, not slowing down until he gave one last thrust and froze. Warm seed filled her. Becca would carry Mike's scent for everyone else to pick up.

She didn't know if that was Mike's plan, but it was hers.

After he pulled out of her, Becca rolled over, then grabbed hold of his shoulders, yanking him down. She latched her mouth to the side of his neck. She'd mark her man in her own way.

* * * *

Mike wiped his hands nervously on his jeans before he knocked on the Alpha's office door. This conversation had been coming for a while and he was more anxious than he thought he'd be.

"Come in."

Mike took a deep breath at the voice on the other side of the door before turning the knob and entering.

"Mike!" Alpha Nelson greeted. "Come in, come in."

"I was hoping you'd have a minute."

Alpha Nelson was a big guy and he'd never been as intimating as he was in that moment. Shit, this was ridiculous. Mike had been up against armed terrorists who hadn't had him shaking in his boots.

"For you, always." Alpha Nelson pushed back from his desk then stood. "Would you like a coffee? I had a carafe sent in earlier."

Since he'd come to the Alpha before Becca or anyone else was awake, Mike appreciated the gesture. "Yes, please."

Alpha Nelson nodded as he strolled over to the small wet bar in the corner. Mike glanced around the large office, noticing how many pictures there was of Becca with her dad and other members of the Pack. He settled some, knowing that he was making the right decision.

He startled when the Alpha put a hand on his shoulder.

"Easy," Alpha Nelson said. "I'm picking up on some tension. Whatever it is bothering you, we'll work it out. You're part of our family now."

"Really?" Mike squeaked. He quickly cleared his throat. "I mean, that's sort of what I wanted to talk to you about."

"Sit down, relax," Alpha Nelson pointed at the couch. "Let's talk."

Mike shuffled, following behind until he had to sit on the plush leather couch. Alpha Nelson sat in one of the overstuffed chairs in front of him then sipped from his mug. Mike took a sip, letting the caffeine and flavor burst over his tongue and calm his nerves. All he had to do was ask for what he wanted. It would benefit the Pack. He knew that Becca, Todd and Kenny wanted him to stay. It was practically a done deal. He needed the Alpha to accept him.

If Mike wasn't involved with the Alpha's daughter, the question wouldn't be so important. Well, if he wasn't falling in love with Becca then he wouldn't even be asking, so a double-edged sword.

Mike drained about half his cup, letting the liquid burn down his throat before straightening his shoulders. He looked Alpha Nelson in the eye. "I would like to formally ask permission to stay in your territory."

Alpha Nelson pressed his lips together, while wrinkling his brow. "For how long?"

"I'm sorry?" Mike asked. That wasn't the reaction he'd expected.

"How long would you like to stay? Are we talking a few weeks? A month? Until all threats against the pack have been taken care of?"

"I... um, I didn't have an actual length in mind," Mike managed.

"It would be highly unusual for an Alpha to allow a strong wolf such as yourself to remain with his Pack without knowing his full intentions," Alpha Nelson stated.

"Intentions?" Mike repeated.

The Alpha nodded. "Let me ask you a question. Your answer will affect my decision."

Holy shit! Mike swallowed back the curse. He'd been nervous before, but now he was sweating. Would the Alpha not let him stay? What would he tell Becca? They'd have to work out how to see each other. There was no way that Mike was going to let her go. His entire future would eventually wrap around her. "Okay."

"Are you staying for the Pack or Becca?"

That was an easy question. "Becca," he said. "But I do want the Pack protected. That's a part of who I am. If I stay, I have to be a part of watching over everyone."

"You can stay on one condition," Alpha Nelson said.

Mike's pulse jumped. "And that is?"

"When you and Becca decide to make your relationship a more permanent arrangement, it's done here. I understand I might lose her to your Pack one day, but I want her here for as long as possible."

Before the Alpha even finished speaking, Mike was shaking his head. "I wouldn't ask her to leave this Pack. In fact, if and when she agrees to be mine, I'll request to join yours."

"It's typical for the female to join with the male's Pack," Alpha Nelson pointed out.

"Well, we both know that Becca's not typical," Mike joked.

The Alpha lifted a brow. He wasn't going to let Mike out of the conversation without further explanation.

"I don't go home because I'm not comfortable in my own Pack." He sighed. "I've seen a lot in my travels. There're Packs that are powerful, like mine, that care only about appearances. They wouldn't ever help another Pack in need unless they get something in return. I'm not saying that the Alpha is wrong on how he reigns, but that's not how I want to live my life. Or how I want my children raised."

"Children?" Alpha clapped his hands together. "Now, we're talking."

Mike laughed. The relief flooded in, and he could lean back. "Not for a while. But in the future? I could see a few pups running around here."

The smile on Alpha Nelson's face was huge. "You know the head of security position will probably be coming available," he said.

"I've discussed it with Kenny," Mike admitted.

"Then all I have to say is welcome to the family." Alpha Nelson held out his hand.

Mike shook it. "Thanks, Alpha." Okay, now that Mike could breathe again, he'd enjoy his coffee before going up to wake Becca.

"Should I expect a call from your Alpha?"

Mike laughed. "No, he doesn't care what I do. My mother is a whole other issue, but she should leave you alone since you're an Alpha. I'm going to have to take Becca to meet them."

"That shouldn't be so bad."

"As long as they don't run her off. My family might act cultured and sophisticated, but they can be real mean at times," Mike explained.

"Trust Becca to be able to handle herself," Alpha Nelson said. "She's been working Pack politics all her life. She's the Pack Daughter for a reason."

Mike hadn't considered that. "That's good to know."

"Becca's received advanced training on how to handle situations. I'd bet on her against your mother on any day of the week." There was pride in the Alpha's tone.

"I guess we'll see," Mike said.

The desk phone rang, causing a short grunt from the Alpha. Mike guessed it was time for to let the man work. He stood then held out his hand. Now that he was staying with permission, he did need to make the call home he'd been avoiding.

Mike had been planning on driving up to his parents to attend whatever social engagement they'd decided he needed to attend before hauling ass back to Becca. If Alpha Nelson was correct, maybe he should take Becca.

He strolled out of the room, digging into his pocket to get his cell. Mike waited until he'd walked through the house and was out on the back porch before he dialed the number of his parents' house.

"Hello, Mike," his mother greeted. "It's about time you returned my call. I've phoned all your friends, trying to reach you."

"I wish you'd stop doing that," Mike said. "I get your messages. I always return your call when I can."

"Well, how do I know you haven't been killed and no one informed us? I'm your mother, after all."

Mike would have felt guilty if he didn't know the next words that would be coming out of her mouth.

"If you came home and took your place at your father's side, I wouldn't have to worry. But no, you insist on running around the world trying to be a hero."

"I'm not trying to be a hero," Mike said. "I want to help people."

His mother humphed. Mike was not going to start this old argument again when he had Becca naked and in bed waiting on him.

"Is there a specific reason you were trying to reach me?" he asked, even though he knew.

"Your presence is required at home this weekend," she stated. "Your father, the Alpha, has some very important people coming."

"Fine," Mike said. "I'll be there."

"Really?" His mom sounded surprised. "Well, of course you will. This is what is expected."

Mike rolled his eyes even though she wouldn't be able to see him. "I'll be bringing a guest," he informed her.

"I don't believe this is an event your fellow…soldiers will be comfortable at. Maybe you can leave them behind for once. For your family."

Since Mike wasn't any more comfortable than the few friends he'd ever taken to meet his family, he merely spoke over her. "It's a date. The woman who I'm dating will be coming with me. I'm sure she'll be an acceptable addition."

"Well, how was I to know?" his mother complained. "You haven't told me that you're dating and you've never brought a woman home in a long time."

Because his mother had been so horrible that he'd finally stopped subjecting those he cared for to her. "Well, I'm bringing someone, so I expect you to be nice."

His mother sputtered in outrage.

"Save it, Mother," he said.

"Who is this girl? What family is she from? How do you know she's not with you because of who your family is?" The questions, the same ones as always, came rapid fire.

"You'll meet her when she arrives," Mike said. "That's all you need to know." He'd made the mistake of giving his parents information beforehand and his father had actually 'investigated' his dates.

"I don't see why you always have to be so difficult," she said. "I'm merely looking out for the family."

"You're looking out for your best interests, not mine. It doesn't matter this time, because nothing you do or say will make a difference." Mike was certain that Alpha Nelson was right about Becca. She wasn't the type of woman to allow another to intimate her.

"Then I look forward to meeting this mystery woman."

"I'm sure you do," Mike stated. "What night is this party?"

"Saturday. It starts at six."

"We'll be there in the afternoon," he said.

"Fine. I'll have a room prepared. I suppose you'll be sharing?"

"We will," Mike agreed. "I'll see you in a few days." He hung up before she could draw him into another argument. This was about the time that she'd begin to pressure him into committing to staying home for good. After the party, he'd sit both his mom and dad down to explain that he would be joining Becca's Pack one day. They wouldn't be happy, but there wouldn't be anything they could do, either.

Mike pocketed his phone before turning back to the house. He liked the main house, but he was looking forward to returning to Becca's cottage, the two of them.

There was still no sign of anyone else being awake as he crept down the halls. Other than a small kitchen staff, all the shifters were still nice and warm in their beds. Like his lover.

He quietly moved up the stairs until he was standing in front of the guest room he'd first been given. He assumed that Becca had her own room somewhere inside the big place, but she hadn't mentioned it. They would be moving back to the cottage later that day, hopefully, so he guessed it didn't matter.

Mike pushed open the door and peeked inside.

Becca was still sound asleep, but she'd grabbed his pillow and placed it under her chin. Mike grinned. She seemed to like his scent. That pleased Mike more than it should.

He crept inside, making sure to close the door silently before strolling across the room. Mike slipped out of the clothes he'd thrown on earlier. Once naked, he lifted the sheet before slipping in next to Becca. She didn't even move.

Well, he was going to have to wake her up his own way.

Mike shifter closer until his chest pressed against her back. Becca murmured in her sleep before pushing back.

He slipped a hand around her body. He brushed his fingers from her stomach until he cupped her breast.

"Mike," she whispered.

"Good morning," he said in her ear.

"It is now," she agreed. Becca covered his hand with hers before tightening the grip. She gasped then pushed back against him again.

His erection slipped between her thighs.

Mike moved his hips in lazy thrusts. Just brushing against her skin was enough for his body to spark.

Becca reached back then gripped his shaft. Her stroke was firm and perfect. Mike shoved his cock through her fist until pre-cum started to leak.

With a firm hand, he lifted up her leg. He wanted, no *needed*, to fill her again. He could still pick up the scent of his cum from the previous night and it was driving him crazy.

It was Becca who positioned his hard-on at her entrance.

He pushed the tip inside.

Mike had enjoyed the rough and passionate lovemaking last evening, but now he could take his time and show her how he could also gently please her.

Becca gripped his hip as Mike pressed farther. He moved softly in and out of her. She still sang for him. Each gasp, moan and catch of breath had arousal sliding down his spine. It was crazy how close he was to coming already.

"Perfect," she told him. "It's always so good."

Mike kissed the nape of her neck before nibbling down. Becca shuddered then climaxed. The way she clamped down on his shaft was almost painful. He thrust lazily while she shook apart in his arms. With his mouth still on her shoulders, teeth digging, holding her in place but not breaking skin, he let himself go. Coming, marking, claiming her as his.

Chapter Eleven

Mike took a deep breath before ringing the doorbell of his parents' house. Becca's hand was in his as she stood by his side, a strong, solid presence.

"A freakin' mansion," she muttered. "No one said anything about a mansion."

He hid his smile. "I thought I'd mentioned it."

"Liar," she whispered as the door opened.

Mike was surprised to see his mother answering. She hardly ever did tasks that she had staff for.

"I was hoping it was you," his mother said. "You are very late. The party will be starting soon."

"Yes," he agreed. Mike sipped his head. "I'd hoped to leave earlier, but a few things needed our attention before we left."

His mom shifted her gaze from him to Becca.

"Mother, please meet Becca Nelson," he introduced.

"Mrs. Jackson." Becca stepped forward. "You have such a lovely home. Thank you so much for inviting me. It's a real honor."

The surprise on his mother's face was worth the long drive home. He'd never seen his mom speechless before.

"I've never been up this way before," Becca continued. "The trees here are massive. I saw that you have several different ones along the back of the property. With your permission, I'd love for Mike to show them to me later."

There was a slight sputter before his mother recovered. "Well, of course, young lady. I'd be happy for my son to do that. We've kept our landscape native to our area. No tropical or unnatural species."

"It's truly lovely," Becca agreed.

Mike smirked when his mom turned her gaze on his. Alpha Nelson had been on target about bringing Becca. The frown he received from his mother matched her glare.

"Come inside." She ushered them. "I don't want the guests arriving with you still on the doorstep."

They still had an hour, but Mike didn't argue. He laid his hand on Becca's lower back as they stepped forward.

Sometime in his absence, the foyer had been remodeled. Instead of the dark wood he was used to, the space now gleamed white and bright. He approved.

"This looks great," he praised.

His mom turned on her heel. She appeared to be searching his face. For sarcasm, maybe? "You like it?"

"I do," he said. The staircase still took up most of the area, but the new tile, décor and pictures were inviting.

"I had to fight your father on redecorating, but I think it was worth it."

Mike nodded.

"I redid the sitting room, as well. He won't allow me to touch his office, though."

"Well, you have to leave the man his own space," Mike commented. "He barely uses the sitting room, anyway."

"Yes, well…" She straightened her skirt before motioning him toward said room. "Come and I'll have drinks poured. I'm pleased you've dressed for the occasion."

Mike snorted. He would have shown up in jeans and a T-shirt, but Becca had put her foot down. She'd stated that if she was going to dress up, which she was, that he'd do so as well. Becca had even picked out the dark-blue suit he wore. "You can thank Becca."

"I'm sure I can," his mom replied.

The change in the sitting room was as shocking as the one in the foyer had been. Instead of the flower-patterned furniture and sweet-smelling space, Mike found himself in a comfortable, masculine room. Brown leather couches and chairs had replaced the once uncomfortable seating. He whistled in appreciation.

His mom was beaming. Wow, Mike had never seen her like this. Not in his entire life. While she was still acting prim and proper, there had been changes going on. He wondered what else would be in store for him.

"Your father should be coming along."

"I'm here."

Mike turned to greet his dad. He had always seen the resemblance between him and his father and as Mike aged, it was even stronger. There were gray flecks at his dad's temples, but he still held an aura of authority.

"Son, glad you could make it."

He shook his father's hand before motioning to Becca. "Thanks, this is Becca Nelson."

His dad greeted Becca with a friendly shake. "Alpha Nelson's daughter?"

"Yes, sir," she said. "It's a pleasure to meet you."

"Your father is an Alpha?" his mom asked, returning with two glasses of white wine.

Mike would have preferred a beer, but he accepted the glass.

"Yes, ma'am," Becca said.

"Sit, you two," his mother insisted. "Tell us what's been going on."

Mike led Becca to the couch, waiting until she sat, then joined her. He was surprised that his mom asked. Normally this was the time that she'd start in on him returning home and taking over the responsibilities she thought he should. "Why don't you tell them," he suggested to Becca. Mike wanted to watch Becca interact with his parents. They wouldn't be there often, but that moment was his two worlds coming together.

Becca was his future, while his parents held his past memories. He wasn't as close to them as he'd like. The constant pressure made him stay away. *What would it be like to come home, though, and not fight with my family?*

As Becca went through the events that had been taking place, Mike watched his parents. His father must have already heard some of the story, because he knew what questions to ask. His mom, on the other hand, looked horrified.

His mother's gaze went to him. "You helped?"

"Mike was able to save one of my good friends, as well as locate Dan Carter. Without him, I don't know how much damage would have been done. Someone could have really gotten hurt."

"Thank God it's over," his mom stated.

"But it's not," Mike said. "Dan Carter is still out there. The Pack is still in danger."

"You're going back?" his father asked. He was already nodding, though, so Mike knew he wouldn't have to explain.

"Yes."

His mom peered from him to Becca. "For how long?"

Mike hadn't wanted to have this conversation yet. He'd figured there would be plenty of time after the party to let his parents know he eventually planned on joining Becca's Pack. He slipped his hand around Becca's fingers and squeezed.

"For as long as Becca will have me," he answered.

His mother gasped, but his dad laughed. Mike glanced at his father.

"I knew it would take a good woman to finally get you to slow down."

Mike raised an eyebrow. His father had never said much to him. Not since he'd first enlisted in the military. His dad had never served and had told Mike he was making a mistake. Mike had walked away. He'd left the man who had played ball with him in the backyard. The father who'd taught him to swim. For the first time since that day, Mike felt the tie between them again.

"Your mother and I have been discussing your situation," his father said.

"Situation?" Mike asked.

"The fact that you don't plan to come home," his mom said.

Mike sighed. "My place isn't here. I've been trying to tell you that."

His mother pressed her lips into a firm line before nodding. "So your father keeps telling me. I've agreed to stop hounding you about it. I ask that you come home more than twice a year."

If his mom stayed off his back about living back home, Mike had no problem visiting more. Even if it was to attend stupid fancy dinners and parties. As long as Becca remained by his side. "I can make more of an effort," he conceded. "If you stop asking when I'm coming home, I'll visit more often."

"Then it's a deal," his mom stated. She rose. "Now I need to make certain everything is ready for this evening."

Becca stood, as well. "Can I help?"

His mom nodded once. "That is acceptable. I will give you a tour while we're at it."

"That'd be great," Becca said. "This house is huge."

"I'm sure you have a large residence, as well. Your father is Alpha of a good-size Pack."

"I didn't grow up in anything like this, though," Becca said, as they walked out of the room.

Mike looked over to his dad. "I feel like I've entered the *Twilight Zone*."

"It hasn't been easy, but your mother is coming around at last. She's known that you weren't going to join the family business, but she still thinks she needs to push you. I've finally made her see that she's been pushing you away."

"She wasn't the only one," Mike said. He didn't want to fight with his dad, but there were a lot of issues that needed to be addressed.

"I made mistakes. I thought you would end up dead in place far from home. I've seen too many of our people killed to want that for my son. I grew up in a different time from you. When I was graduating high school, we had a draft that we worried about."

"I know. But I knew that was where I was meant to be. I'm not like you or my brother. I don't want to wear suits every day and sit behind a desk."

His dad smiled. "We do a little more than that, but I understand. Or at least I'm trying to."

"Why all this change of heart?" Mike didn't want to be suspicious, but this was all of his dreams coming true. Having Becca, a future in a Pack and now his parents treating him like an adult.

His father glanced toward the hall then leaned forward. "I've received several phone calls this past week."

"About me?" he asked.

"Alpha Nelson phoned first. Then a member of the Alpha Council. After that a sheriff from some town in New Mexico. A lot of people wanted me to know that you've been helping others."

Mike smiled. He appreciated that his friends had cared enough to get involved, but he was scared to hope that this new attitude would last. "And the redecorating?"

His father smiled. "We're going to be grandparents. Your brother is expecting his first pup. It's given your mom a new outlook on a lot of things. I don't think I would have been able to convince her to back off without this new turn."

"I'm going to be an uncle. That's awesome." He wasn't close to his brother, but maybe now that his relationship with his parents might be better, he could try with his siblings.

"Maybe," his father said, "we'll have more than one grandpup running around her soon."

He laughed. "Give us time before you start pressuring us for kids, please."

"I'll try, but your mother has the bug."

Mike couldn't believe how different this visit was compared to what he'd been expecting. He was enjoying talking to his dad.

"Let's go see if we can help."

"Sure." He followed his dad out of the sitting room. They walked down the long hall until they reached the entrance to the kitchen. Mike stopped and stared.

His mother, the woman he thought was cold and hard, had her head back laughing at something Becca said. He'd never seen his mom like that before.

Mike leaned against the door jamb. He smiled. It seemed like the Pack Daughter had the ability to bring more than her own people together.

Becca glanced up and noticed him. "Hey!" she said. "Your mom told me she's going to be a grandma. Isn't that great?"

"It is," Mike agreed. He pushed off the wall to stroll forward. "I'll totally be the cool uncle."

She wrapped her arm around his waist once he'd reached her. Mike took her weight, holding her close. Before the house filled up with strangers and people he didn't care about, Mike would enjoy being home, finally. Home, which was what Becca was to him.

Whether in her Pack territory or his, she was all he needed.

Want to see more from this author?
Here's a taster for you to enjoy!

Birds of Prey
Crissy Smith

Excerpt

Cody Johnson disconnected the call on his cell phone and started to pace the floor of his new office area. He'd spent the last week setting up the room that would, starting today, belong to him and his team.

He appreciated the call from his contact with the Wolf Shifter Council, Kurt Moore, to wish him luck in his new position. For several months he'd waited while arrangements were made so he could begin work. He was anxious to finally get started.

He breathed deeply. His office and his team's workplace were exactly as he'd wanted. Four large desks were pushed into the middle of the room, all facing one another. Laptops and other devices, waiting to be used, sat atop the surfaces.

Wide windows covered the north wall of the building and let in plenty of natural light. Every part of him approved of the open view. Inside himself, the falcon part of him loved the fact that he was surrounded by lots of room and space.

Just left of the windows hung several monitors. Any team member would be able to connect with a screen and share its data. Across from that, on the other end of the room, Cody had a state-of-the-art break area. The best appliances and provisions were available for late nights and early mornings. The remaining wall on the south side of the room was covered with white boards and bulletin boards. The double doors to enter were thick and solid.

It had taken time and a lot of money to set up the local branch of the Shifter Coalition, but it had been worth it. The need for the alliance and a branch of law enforcement for shifters had pushed for everyone to move quickly in setting up the brand new Coalition.

The Lake Worth division was located in an old brick building, set in the middle of town and twenty minutes from the lake shore.

The tall structure was three stories and consisted of a reception area, gym, interview rooms and holding cells on the bottom level. The second floor was where Cody's area was, along with several other shifter species teams. The top story was reserved for the highest officials and conference rooms for meetings and guests.

The Coalition was organized and motivated.

Nine months after the first of the shifters had announced their presence to the world, the Coalition would now serve to protect and police all shifters. Thanks to the Alpha Wolf Council who'd first come up with the idea of a combined alliance, the Coalition had been born.

Cody was pleased to have been asked to be involved. He'd served ten years with the elite Army Rangers before he'd become a homicide detective in Phoenix for the last seven years.

But it wasn't his military record or his place on the force that had gained him the attention of the Council. No, he had been involved in the rescue of a friend that had landed him in the path of the wolf shifter who had first come up with the vision of an alliance.

Kurt Moore had helped hand-pick some of the division leaders. Cody, Zak and Jamie had all been offered contracts with the Coalition. All three men had accepted.

The added bonus of the Coalition setting up in his home town of Lake Worth, Arizona, had been too good to pass up. He was home. After too many years away, it was good to be back.

He'd gladly accepted his new position — team leader of the Birds of Prey division.

As a falcon shifter, Cody used his changing ability as often as he could. He loved to transform, but that wasn't the only reason. Bird shifters had sharper eyesight in and out of their animal form.

Each shifter species had enhanced senses, although not all enhancement was the same. While wolves possessed heightened scent, birds relied a lot on their vision.

Before the shifters had become public, Cody hadn't had the same freedom to shift as he did now.

Shifters were larger and stronger than their natural bird cousins. If anyone had seen Cody in his other form, the chance of someone finding out what he truly was would have been worrisome. There was no way that anyone would have believed that shifter birds were natural. As his animal, he was more than twice the size, very strong and hard to injure.

Bird shifters weren't the only team that were a part of the Coalition, though. There were wolves, felines, bears, coyotes, and so many more shifters in the world.

Already he'd met several other team leaders and found them to be just as dedicated to the security goals as he.

Dossiers on his team members had been provided, and judging from the extensive reports he'd been reviewing, he was impressed. While he still hadn't met any of his squad, that situation would change shortly. He'd only spoken to each one on the phone as the final preparations had been made for their unit to begin work.

He strolled across the room to pour a cup of coffee from the pot he'd started earlier. He was keyed up to begin working and had to call on all his training to remain calm. Even with the years of experience, it was difficult.

Cody settled himself at the desk he'd commandeered for himself and pulled out the files for his new team.

Ryder Evans—red-tailed falcon. Ryder's picture showed a lean, athletic, tall man with light-brown hair, almost blond in some streaks, and light-colored eyes. He smiled easily at the camera, showing off a dimple in his left cheek. He was an instructor for the US Marine Corps Special Forces teams. His specialty was hand-to-hand combat and other fighting forms.

The next member was Byron Ward. Byron was a golden eagle, which was the most popular bird of prey but also the most unique shifter. While golden eagles in nature outnumbered all the other bird species, in shifters they were very rare. No one seemed to know why.

Byron had transferred to them from the Las Vegas Metro Police after ten years on the force. Byron's picture was of a big guy with lots of muscles. His dark-brown hair and deep, dark eyes stared into the camera without a hint of a smile. His superiors described him as intense and focused. Cody hoped that remained true.

He closed Byron's file and picked up the last one.

Chloe Diaz. Chloe was only five foot five and very slim. She had been an analyst with the FBI for over twelve years. Chloe's animal was a burrowing owl.

After Cody had received her information, he'd had to dig into the shifter database about that class of birds. He'd never come across one before. The burrowing owl shifters were almost non-existent and even with Cody's high security clearance, he couldn't find much on the species.

Her expertise in analyzing intel would really benefit the team. He had high hopes that she would fit in with the others.

A knock on the door interrupted his thoughts. He shuffled all the folders inside a desk drawer and leaned back in his chair.

"Come in," he called out.

The two men who entered were easily recognized.

Cody stood and held out his hand. "Cody Johnson."

"Ryder Evans," Ryder replied and gave his hand a firm shake.

"Byron," the second man announced in a deep, rumbling voice.

"Welcome, gentlemen." Cody waved them forward.

The door was still open when he glimpsed movement behind Byron and Ryder.

"Please come in," he invited Chloe.

He greeted her then took a look at his squad. Yes, he believed the four of them would accomplish a lot.

He motioned toward the desks. "Let's get started."

About the Author

Crissy Smith lives in Texas with her husband, daughter, and three Labrador retrievers. The three dogs love to curl up under her computer desk and nap while she writes. It doesn't leave a lot of room for her but what's a woman to do?

When not writing or reading, she enjoys hunting, camping and shooting. But she has a girly side too and is addicted to pedicures and coffee.

She has been writing since she was a teenager and still loves everything to do with the paranormal. Her stories and characters all have a place in her heart. She loves the Alpha male, the dominant werewolf, and the Master vampire, which find their way in most of her books.

Learn more about the characters she has created at her website where they have their very own page. It will be updated from time to time to let you know what's going on with them. Also you can find out who will be in the next book.

Crissy loves to hear from readers. You can find her contact information, website details and author profile page at http://www.totallybound.com.

TOTALLY
BOUND

Home of Erotic Romance